RETURN TO OBAN:

Anna's Next Chapter

RUTH HAY

About This Book

Return to Oban: Anna's Next Chapter *is the seventh story in the* ***Prime Time*** *series.*

Anna Mason Drake has seen many changes in her life. She returns to Oban once more, expecting a peaceful time among her friends.

Will she find the respite she longs for, or another set of demanding challenges to be faced?

———

"Anything is possible. Stay open, forever, so open it hurts, and then open up some more, until the day you die, world without end, amen."

George Saunders

Chapter One

Most days it was all right; or almost all right. Most days she could forget the loss and concentrate on the many gains. After all, whether she was in Canada or in Scotland, she could count on old and beloved friends for company and support. How many women of her age could say the same? She was blessed in so many ways. Except one.

Lawren was gone and the loss was just as huge now, as on the day, years before, when he died.

Of course, she could not go around moaning and complaining about the loss when so many others in the world had much more to worry about. When so many had lost children, or jobs, or their very homeland from wars and disasters for which the sufferers were never to blame.

Anna Mason Drake acknowledged all this and kept her mouth shut and her head up. Most days.

But in the dark, lonely night when she awoke and turned to seek warmth and comfort and found only an empty space, she lay awake and bereft.

How could it be that she had found the perfect man after giving up all hope of a fulfilling relationship and then lost him too soon?

Why did she hesitate to commit to him and waste all that time they could have spent together?

What difference had it made in the end that Lawren was several years her junior?

Why didn't she jump into his arms the first time he made his feelings known to her?

Was it her failure with Richard that had caused such caution? If so, who cared? Richard was part of her youth, her inexperience, and he too was gone.

In the darkest moments she dreaded the thought that she would never again feel the strong arms of a man who loved her above all things. And yet, when the sun shone and the day was clear and cool with trees and flowerbeds in full bloom, she knew how lucky she had been to be loved at all by a man as special as Lawren Drake.

The world knew him as a consummate artist. A painter who could draw out of his human subject's feelings and emotions they hardly knew existed. A portrait painter whose work had spoken to Anna's heart the first time she saw it on the walls of a legal office boardroom in London, Ontario. She had not realized it then, but she later discovered his psychic ability to see the future in the faces of even young children. Liam and Annette were evidence of this. The children were now verging on their teen years and yet, the McLennan family portrait Lawren had completed when they were little ones, contained the essence of the young adults they were becoming in the present.

Anna had the ultimate evidence of this magical ability in her bedroom upstairs in the McCaig Estate Farmhouse in Oban. Lawren had created a large canvas showing three generations of McLeod women arranged in such a way that they were interconnected even although he had not met two of the generations and never knew the places he had hinted at in the background.

It was the one solace Anna had. She wished she might have it with her wherever she went but it was perfectly placed above the fireplace in their Scottish house and it would have risked damage to the priceless work to trail it around the world whenever she went on a plane.

And yet, the impulse to re-visit the portrait grew stronger the longer she was in Canada. It felt like coming home to be within sight of it again, but there was a reverse side to proximity, for this room was where they had lived and loved together in their happiest hours and there, eventually, was where she felt the most alone.

There was no answer to this quandary. The bottom line was simply that she missed Lawren Drake and always would.

Chapter Two

"All right then, Anna. I know what's going on. I may not be able to *see* perfectly, but I can always tell when you are getting itchy to go back to Oban again."

Alina crossed the floor of her immaculate sitting room, kept clear of obstructions by her watchful husband Philip, and stood in front of Anna so she could not be ignored.

"I don't know where you get this idea from, Alina. I thought I was disguising it very well but I guess you have known me the longest of anyone and that gives you privileges, in addition to keen insights into my habits. What do you think about the idea?"

"I think, I wish I could come with you to Scotland again but Philip has work here in London advising the local council on the plans for the renewal of The Forks of the Thames River. He won't budge till he is satisfied the plan is good enough in all respects. I can't leave for several months, I suspect, and I don't think you will wait that long. Am I right?"

"Possibly. Is the house occupied at the moment?"

Alina turned to the desk where her computer stood at the ready. Its enlarged screen and extra-large print enabled her to keep track of the family members, or the renters, who stayed occasionally in the charming estate house when Anna did not need it. Alina also supervised operations of their business,

A Plus Knitwear; an online shopping experience supplying a wide variety of knitted goods to customers all over the world.

It took only a minute before she responded. "No occupants at the moment, Anna. Jeanette is scheduled to do a house inspection in a week or so but I doubt she'll be able to manage it with the move to their new house imminent in about a month. They need more space now her mother, Jean, is coming from Vancouver to live with them. Jean will help out with the children since Jeanette's Design business has grown. Jeanette will probably ask one of her employees to do the inspection instead."

"So I could go any time?"

"If you want to be there for the birth of Fiona's third it would be good timing, I think. You could hardly miss that big event. Now Gordon is the Laird of Glenmorie it will be a feather in his cap if they can produce another son."

Anna laughed out loud. "The Border Campbells will be green with envy! All Gordon's sisters can produce are girls, and more girls, but perhaps our Fiona would rather have another girl in the castle this time, for company?"

"You can ask her by phone, of course, but I feel sure you would rather be there."

Anna smiled and nodded her head. Then she became serious and it showed in her voice at once.

"Alina, I know you can't travel without Philip or me, and I am truly wondering how much longer I can do that flight across the Atlantic. Surely, by now, the airlines should have a faster method to power their engines. I thought the age of the Jetsons would be here by now and save us all the time and trouble of airports and overnight flights."

Alina chuckled. "Dream on, my dear! Just be glad you won't have to pack more than a carry-on for your trip. That's the advantage of having your own house to go to, with extra clothes stored in the locked cedar closet above the main entrance."

"I suppose you're right. It's easier for me than for many others I see on those planes with children and toys and piles of extra luggage to deal with. At least I can get out of the plane and on my way quickly once I get there."

"And don't forget how lucky you are to be able to afford to travel First Class nowadays. That really makes a big difference."

Anna agreed. She knew if she ever needed a substantial amount of cash she could sell one of Lawren's paintings. He had not lived long enough to supply the art world with hundreds of pieces, so demand was high for those that remained in Anna's care. The trouble was that she thought of these as his children and was reluctant to part with any one of them.

A silence fell, and both women knew the unspoken question was whether Anna would decide to live out her last years in Canada, with her oldest friend and her husband, Philip, who was Anna's half-brother, or in Scotland with three other Samba members and a large contingent of friends and knitters in the area, not to mention an entirely new branch of McLeods now centred in Glasgow.

It was not an urgent predicament as long as Anna was hale and hearty. Alina's vision problems had impacted her life, although the Macular Degeneration Research Program from London's Ivey Institute had lessened the effects of her disability. And yet, an enormous and vital part of her life would disappear if Anna decided to stay in Scotland beyond the point where she could comfortably travel back to Canada again. There was nothing to compare to the companionship of old friends who knew each other's lives and troubles and who could often finish each other's sentences.

Both women had been born and raised in London, Ontario. In their foreign travels they had come to appreciate the convenience and ease of Canadian living. In recent years, seniors' retirement homes of various kinds had sprung up nearby, providing an alternative to living alone in their advanced years should the need arise, but this had to be an individual and last-ditch choice.

Alina knew this, but she would never put any pressure on Anna. That was not the role of an old friend.

It had taken Anna Mason Drake many years to come into her own and to make good decisions for herself. Alina must trust in these decisions and be content with whatever happened.

It's not going to be soon! She reassured herself. *Take each day as it comes and be grateful.*

With this admonition in her head, Alina turned the conversation to other matters.

"So, Maria and Paul have bought a big home in Andover Trails? It was always a dream of theirs to watch the geese return each evening to the big pond and to be able to walk around the pathways throughout the subdivision."

"The location suits them very well. It's so close to major shopping outlets now. Southdale Road is a great, fast road to downtown or White Oaks Mall but the traffic noise is dampened by the number of trees and plants around their subdivision. Maria seems happy with the choice."

"I think she wanted a big yard for her grandkids to play in and also a lower level office so she can watch them while she keeps an eye on her fashion business."

"Don't you love how things work out, Alina? Who would have predicted young Lucy would have made such a name for herself in the film industry? She's out in Vancouver again doing costumes for some science fiction/fantasy series. She really does have her mother's and grandmother's skills at her fingertips. I imagine Hollywood will be calling before long. Any word of a romance?"

"Not that I have heard. I'm sure Maria would be on the phone as soon as *that* news broke!"

They laughed together in a comfortable way as friends do who know the peculiarities and hopes of their other friends. The Samba group had been a stalwart support over many years. Now that Susan was on her own, the three remaining London originals met frequently to check up on each other. There was a special sympathy between Anna and Susan because of their shared widowhood although both acknowledged the difference between the long goodbye of Susan's Jake, compared to the very sudden loss of Anna's Lawren. None the less, they each had to adjust to the 'empty house' syndrome and often commented on ways to fill their time and their space.

Anna had emptied Lawren's old downtown studio and taken his paintings to the Rosecliffe condo where they were now displayed on every wall that could accommodate them.

When Philip had pointed out how this made her condo a target for thieves, she had installed a state-of-the-art security system that not only alerted the security company and the police of any intruders, but also sent a signal to Alina and Philip just two doors away. Their home had an outdoor camera tied to the system which would capture the image of a stranger even if he, or she, had managed to disarm the main system at Anna's.

Susan had decided to remain in the house she had shared with Jake despite the memories that haunted her. She had signed up with the local hospital to offer temporary accommodation to out-of-town patients who required wheelchair access during treatment. There was one proviso. She still had one large retriever dog at home and he had his own space near Susan upstairs. As it turned out, this became an advantage since Dominic was trained by Jake to provide help to a wheelchair occupant and he often assisted in pulling a heavy chair up the outside ramp during icy weather.

Anna did not have the same space to fill in her condo. It

had only two bedrooms, one of which was now an office. The space she needed to fill was in the area of time; long days without a purpose lay heavy on the heart. Too much time to regret her losses was damaging to her self-esteem and she did not want to be required to re-establish her sense of self, so hard won many years ago when Helen Dunlop had come into her life.

Anna had tried returning to her Public Library work at the Central Branch in a downtown Mall but the staff had changed in the intervening years and she felt too old to start making those connections all over again. Her knowledge of current teen reading habits had lapsed and she was not willing to read the vast quantity of zombie, werewolf and vampire novels that would have brought her up to speed.

Reluctantly, she began to download the books she wanted from Amazon. It was easier and cheaper and since she spent a good amount of time on her computer, it was also convenient. Of course, sitting in bed with an e reader or smartphone in her hand did not have the same comfort as the solid feel of a book, but she could always re-read her old favourites whenever she needed a change. It was another way of vanishing into the past and she was sufficiently aware of the danger so that she rationed her 'old' titles and made a pencil note in the title pages whenever she returned for a reading revisit.

Her current computer targets consisted of sourcing ideas for A Plus knitters. More than once when their business was in its infancy, Alina and Anna had managed to jump ahead of the fashion trends and supply their customers with well-made versions of styles that were just coming into public attention.

At first this was luck, but experience had taught them the value of scouring the internet for popular blogs and online designers who created most of the trends. Anna was amazed at how many teenage girls were online with make-up, hair and dress tips. They had astonishing numbers of adherents who followed their advice with enthusiasm.

Despite the age disparity, Anna enjoyed the sheer versatility and ingenuity of these fresh-faced girls who knew their audience well and catered to the lack of money of most of their followers. Watching the bloggers convert older garments into new styles was the inspiration she needed to recommend ideas to Alina and the bands of knitters they maintained on both sides of the Atlantic. It had even become the 'in' thing for young people to knit for themselves. Hollywood actors and actresses began the trend and many now swore by the relaxing feeling of knitting. The click-clack of needles was popular, also, in waiting rooms and hospitals across North America. What these beginners lacked, of course, was the expertise to incorporate patterns and designs into their knitting. For the present, at least, experts like the Scottish Fairisle knitters could devise and adapt patterns and complete new items at incredible speeds the newcomers to the craft could never surpass.

Anna was able to take a quick photo from the internet on her smartphone when she saw an innovative idea and pass the photos on to the knitting teams. With their approval, the automatic knitting machines could be programmed for the less complex parts of the style and hand-knitted designs could be grafted on to complete the effect. It was a winning combination. As long as they could provide new products A Plus would continue to be a viable source for the fashion-conscious woman of any age.

This research required a great deal of Anna's time and for that she was pleased. Sinking into bed at night was satisfactory when her mind was tired from seeking and searching, and sleep came easily most nights.

Alina kept track of Anna's work hours and often protested that she would grow fat and unhealthy if she did not balance her sedentary activities with something more active. She tried to accustom herself to a standing computer desk but found it distracted her from the screen. It went back to the big box store within a week and Alina's next idea for Anna to work while on a moving treadmill was discarded without a trial. The concentrated work of checking into many different blogs online did not allow her to divert her attention to how her feet were performing. She knew she would promptly fall off the moving device and break an arm or leg.

Alina continued to insist. Next on the list was a health club membership for Anna. She tried it for a trial month but found the majority of members to be young, lithe types who made her feel ancient. The machines in the gym looked like medieval torture implements and the entire atmosphere with its grinding music did not suit her one little bit.

"Enough!" she declared. "I promise to walk every day instead. If I walk downhill to Springbank Park and stay on the pathways there by the river, that will have to do. If I can make it back here on the uphill stretch and still breathe, it will be enough."

Alina agreed. She volunteered to keep Anna company on her jaunts and they were able to extend the exercise time by a few minutes each week during the summer months until they were both managing the return hill without collapsing in exhaustion. Philip joined them sometimes. He had discovered the park some years before and was always extolling its virtues.

"You two Londoners don't appreciate what is on your doorstep. It's an exceptionally beautiful park for a city of London's size. The walking paths are designed to showcase the spectacular trees and down by the river the air is fresh and you can watch ducks and birds, and even canoeists, as you walk. Make use of it while you can."

It was a long, mild, Fall season and so the walking continued several times a week to mutual benefit but now that the first signs of an approaching winter could be seen in the colourful leaves, Anna was indeed becoming restless. She loved Thanksgiving in Canada and enjoyed turkey with all the trimmings as a wonderful feast surpassing Christmas in some ways, since there was no necessity to worry about presents. Not that she had many people to buy for these days. Except, of course, for the children of friends in Scotland and those gifts had to be mailed well ahead of time to be sure of arriving before Christmas Day.

And so, as soon as the turkey had been consumed down to the bones in soup, Anna could resist no longer. It was time to journey back to Oban before the winter snow flew in Canada.

Chapter Three

Closing up the condo was simple. She emptied out the fridge delivering anything useful to Alina, packed a rolling carry-on case, set the security system, locked the front door, and stepped into the limousine taking her to Toronto, knowing Alina and Philip were standing by.

The length of her stay was to be determined by the weather conditions in Canada. Although Scotland's winter could produce cold and snow, neither lasted for too long and the spring pushed through the grass much earlier than in Canada. It was her favourite time of year to snuggle down in her spacious home in a beautiful location where just gazing out of the windows at passing clouds and seabirds occupied delightful hours.

With Bev and Alan nearby and Jeanette and George still in Oban, as well as Fiona and Gordon in their castle not too far away, she felt surrounded by friends whenever she needed company.

In the silence and tranquility of the countryside, she could restore her peace of mind and take comfort from the memories of Lawren that infused the house.

The flight was full. The reserved First Class section of the plane had few seats to allow for more space, but these also were filled. Anna had an aisle seat and an older man was on her left, beside the window.

John introduced himself, chatted politely for a minute or two then promptly went to sleep.

After only a few minutes into the flight, Anna knew sleep, for her, was not going to be easy. In the centre seats to her right was a family of four with the youngest child in her mother's arms. The father and another child were occupied with video games and in-flight television while the young mother coped with a fractious baby.

Babies often had difficulty on take-off with changing pressure which affected their ears but this child did not seem to settle after they were at cruising height. Sympathetic glances were exchanged between Anna and the mother.

"I apologize," she murmured. "Evie has been restless all day. I expected her to sleep all the way to Glasgow."

"Don't worry!" whispered Anna. "If you like, I will take her for a bit while you get some rest."

The young mother seemed embarrassed at this offer and renewed her efforts to calm the baby but after another hour of fruitless attempts, and increasingly annoyed glances from other travellers, she had to give in.

Anna took Evie in her arms and rocked back and forth singing an old lullaby under her breath. The baby's eyes started open in amazement as she looked up into this unfamiliar face. Anna was afraid she would begin crying more loudly than before, but the singing took effect and the weight of the child grew increasingly heavy as she finally relaxed into sleep.

Anna held her hand to the red face in her arms and thought Evie might be overheated. She loosened the blanket around her and eased open the little jacket to allow some cooler air to circulate. Evie's mother was now sleeping peacefully and so were the baby's father and brother. In fact, the whole front section of the plane was taking the chance to rest while the baby was quiet. Anna did the same, closing her eyes and breathing deeply while still rocking the baby whenever she stirred for a second.

The respite did not last long but as soon as the crying began, Evie's mother claimed her again and soon passed the baby over to the father at the other side of the cabin. She smiled in grateful thanks and Anna thought Evie was good preparation for cradling Fiona's new baby, who she hoped to meet while in Oban.

They arrived in Glasgow to a morning of cloud and gentle rain. Anna was among the first to exit the plane and she walked straight through the airport to the customs area. As she was the proud possessor of two passports, she progressed through the UK/EU exit and was in a taxi heading for the city's Central Train Station before she had come fully awake.

The air was fresh and damp and always had, for Anna, the exciting scent of a new place with untold discoveries. She replied to the usual enquiries from the driver and settled down to watch the passing traffic and the buildings old and new flying by on the motorway.

Her train was not arriving at the terminus until 10:00am so Anna asked to be dropped off at the Jurys Inn where she knew she could purchase a delicious breakfast and take a rest before walking up to the nearby station with her rolling case in tow.

Well-fed and with renewed energy she arrive in the enclosed, huge and echoing station precinct in just enough time to find her "quiet" carriage on the platform and spot her reserved seat. Her case fit into the space behind her seat and she was soon divested of her raincoat, her hat, and her shoes, which she kicked off under the table. She had stopped to collect an armful of Scottish newspapers and magazines and with the addition of a large cup of tea, which the attendant promised to refill whenever necessary, Anna Mason Drake knew she had once again returned to the alternative comforts of her second home.

❦

Grant's son, Cameron, met her from the train. "How was your journey, Mrs. Drake? My father sends his regards and hopes you will be seeing him on this trip."

"I will make a point of seeing your father, Cameron. There's no one who can collect gossip better than Grant can. He's always a fast way to catch up on what's been happening in Oban while I've been away."

Cameron laughed; a deep chuckle that began somewhere in his lower chest and burbled up from the depth. "You are surely right about that, Mrs. Drake! He's a magnet for gossip. He keeps in touch by phone now that he's retired from driving. My Mum says he costs them a fortune in phone bills but I'm thinking she's glad it keeps him out of her hair most of the time."

"I'm sure she's right about that. It's a good trade off."

Cameron stowed her case into the back of the big Range Rover and made sure she was seated comfortably in the passenger seat. Before they drove off, Anna asked if they could stop at the supermarket to pick up some supplies.

"Och, you'll not be needing to do that! Mrs. Matthews has stocked up the kitchen for you just the other day before they left for the States."

"Oh, have they gone already? I was hoping to see them before they went."

Bev and Alan were her nearest neighbours at the estate farmhouse and it was always good to catch up with them. Bev insisted she needed a Canadian news and views infusion from Anna whenever she arrived.

"Aye, well, it seems their Eric had some big presentation to do in California and he wanted his parents to be there. It's something to do with a new computer thing he's been working on. I think Mrs. Matthews left you a note."

Anna had to be content with that. Bev and Alan would not be away for too long and they would have plenty of time for long chats by the fireside with some of Bev's delicious scones and cakes to share.

They soon left a rainy Oban behind but not before Anna had taken a good look around. As she had expected, there were no major changes to be seen. It was one of the most comforting things about Scotland. The pace of change seemed much slower here. In Ontario, new buildings went up in a flash, restaurants closed or opened, whole subdivisions appeared so quickly that driving along a once-familiar road could be quite disorienting.

Nothing so uncomfortable occurred here. The road to the mountains was the same as it always had been. It flashed by in the usual way as Cameron showed the driving speed he had learned from his father, but as soon as Bev and Alan's homestead appeared Anna felt her inner excitement grow.

Next to appear over the rise would be her very own, substantial, stone house with its welcoming red door.

To her surprise there was a stream of smoke rising from the chimney. Had Bev turned up the Aga in the kitchen or laid a fire before she left? It was a kind thought but highly unusual to let even a long-lasting peat fire smoulder when no one was living there to supervise it.

She was about to draw Cameron's attention to this when he forestalled her.

"Now, dinna be concerned Mrs. Drake. You have a visitor and I was sworn to secrecy. I hope it's a good surprise for you."

He would say no more, so Anna was left, consumed with

curiosity until she reached the front door, and found her great-niece Ashley in her arms, chattering away at such a rate, Anna could not understand a word she said.

"Oh, forgive me! You must be tired from your long journey and I am keeping you standing on your own doorstep. Let me get your case and I'll explain everything."

Ashley stepped outside to exchange a word of thanks with Cameron, leaving Anna to enter the McCaig Estate Farmhouse on her own.

It had, as ever, the effect of wrapping oneself in a warm shawl. The stone walls provided shelter from westerly winds and the south-facing window in the kitchen captured all the sunshine until sunset each day, providing a bright and welcoming prospect over the garden. She sank down on the padded bench by the window and shrugged off her coat, placing her hand on the spot where Morag, the brown tabby, had preferred to sit. The cat was gone now after a long and happy life.

Anna refused to let any regrets mar this homecoming moment. She gazed around the kitchen, the true heart of the home, and found everything as she had expected with the addition of a kettle burbling on the Aga, a table set with plates and cups and a bowl of wildflowers and spruce clippings. The air was warm from the stove, and the bright sunshine which had emerged when they left Oban town. Anna unbuttoned her cashmere cardigan, took a deep breath, and sat back happily to wait for Ashley's explanations. She knew her first cup of tea in the kitchen would soon follow.

"Right, then, I see you are settled already, Aunt Anna. My grandparents send their love and I have imposed myself on you for two reasons. One is that your brother Simon is awaiting a hip operation and Gran Michelle is having a hard time with him as he won't follow doctor's orders and stay off his feet. She is terrified he will trip and shatter what's left of his hip and she has cleared the house of anything that could get in his way. That includes me, I'm afraid. She gave me my marching orders and I went to Halifax to see my publishers."

"I am sorry about Simon. He never was a good patient, even when we were children. It used to frustrate our mother. Is Donna still staying in Prince Edward Island with them?"

"No, my Mom has a new boyfriend and she has moved in with him to see if they are compatible."

Anna tried to control her left eyebrow that always tilted up when she heard something unexpected. Ashley did not notice, as she was pouring boiling water into a brown betty teapot as she spoke.

Anna was still trying to absorb how many changes had occurred in the last few months since she had been in touch with her brother and his wife. Their move from Alberta to the east coast of Canada had not resulted in much easier contact. In fact, it was more difficult to reach the island than it had been to get on a plane and fly to Alberta. Anna knew she had been lax about visits and now she was hearing about things she should have known.

"So, you said there were two reasons?"

"That's right." Ashley pushed forward plates of tempting scones and two pots of home-made jams that had the labels of Bev's Cottage Kitchen. She was gathering her resources for the next revelation.

While Anna busied herself with butter and knife and tea stirring, Ashley Stanton adjusted her glasses, pushed her fair hair into place off her forehead, and bit her lip. The next minutes had to go well or she had miscalculated badly and this daring idea was a lost cause.

"It starts with my publisher. No, it really starts with Lawren."

Ashley had Anna's full attention now. A reference to her husband was unusual in this context. She waited to see what would emerge.

"You remember how Lawren saw into my secret ambitions

when I first met him? We had a private chat up there on top of Helen's Hill. I was a raw, uncertain teenager but he gave me courage to pursue a writing career. I always felt close to him from that moment on. He was so special to me.

Oh, I didn't mean to trouble you. Please don't be sad, Aunt Anna."

She reached forward with a tissue from her pocket but Anna waved away the gesture saying, "I am just so happy to hear you speak of him in this way, Ashley. I know he had an influence on many people and it brings him closer whenever he is mentioned so lovingly. Thank you."

"Oh, the thanks are all mine, believe me! After he died so suddenly, I know you were bombarded with requests to provide comments and do interviews for magazines and art publications. The fact that you chose me for an exclusive, personal and private interview was the real start of my career in journalism.

You do know I am eternally grateful to you for that privilege."

Ashley gulped and swallowed when she saw Anna's reaction. She was determined to proceed with her plan and breaking down in tears was not going to get her there.

"This lengthy preamble brings me, at last, to the second reason. My publisher wants me to write something about Lawren. Before you protest, he was not specific on how or in what format. He is well aware of your reticence to speak of private matters. He knows of our relationship, of course, but he has left it up to me to approach you with the idea and I am totally ready to abandon the whole thing if it is not what *you* want to do."

Ashley stopped and breathed out. The latter statements had come in a rush because of her apprehension. She was banking a great deal on this request but she knew it might well prove fruitless.

Anna was shocked and it showed.

She turned away to look out of the big picture window to

gather her thoughts. Ashley was a dear young woman. She had come to Oban several times when Lawren was here with Anna and again after he had gone. She was good company, a trusted family member and a talented journalist.

The question was whether or not Anna was ready to share with the public in general, aspects of her precious private life and her personal memories of Lawren Drake. Perhaps she would not be so reluctant to consider the request if they had been blessed with a typical decades-long marriage. Their all-too-short time together seemed all the more treasured. She clung to each moment.

And yet, as time passed, she knew some of those moments were beginning to grow dim. She would never feel as if she owed the public access to those memories but it could be that, as guardian of much of Lawren's legacy, she owed the story to her family above all.

If, like Lawren, she should die unexpectedly, there would be few left alive who could tell what she alone knew to be true. The thought of some hack delving into obscure records and pasting together an unauthorized biography at some time in the future, made her skin crawl with distaste.

If it should ever be done at all, Ashley Stanton, her great-niece, Simon's granddaughter, was clearly the writer to do it.

When she turned back to face Ashley, she saw the genuine concern for her aunt in the young woman's anxious expression. Anna believed she had meant it when she promised to drop the entire idea should her great-aunt disapprove.

Suddenly, the decision was made. Now was the perfect time, and now was the perfect place.

"Dear Ashley. I think I have resisted long enough. I trust you, in the love you have for my late husband and for me, to record our story with sensitivity and discretion. We have a lot to discuss, of course, but I am feeling very tired at the moment and I must go to bed. We'll talk tomorrow."

Ashley quickly damped down her elation and contented herself with a gentle hug around her aunt's shoulders. Inside, she was jumping with joy but now was not the time to show it. It had clearly been a difficult decision. A good night's sleep would be the best preparation for a serious discussion about how to collect the information and what was to be included. For the present she restricted herself to one heartfelt 'thank you' then escorted Anna upstairs to her bedroom where a peat fire was burning and fresh sheets were waiting for the weary traveller. While Anna was in the bathroom across the hall, Ashley placed a glass of water by the bedside, closed the drapes and lit a lamp on the bedside table. When everything was in place she went back downstairs and hugged the good news to herself. There was no need to tell her publisher yet. It was still a secret and she intended to keep it as such for as long as she could. Whatever happened in the next weeks in the McCaig Estate Farmhouse near Oban would remain between the two people mostly closely concerned.

Chapter Four

It was not the peaceful night she had hoped for when she turned out the light and snuggled down in the big bed. Hours had gone by when she found herself awake again.

Moonlight had managed to filter through the closed drapes and send a beam over to the painting above the fireplace. It appeared even more magical in the subtle blue light than even in its usual daylight appearance.

Anna's mind was drawn back to the day it was first hung in place; the day and the hour when she realized how special the younger artist was. She had to acknowledge, in that moment, any person who could see into her heart's desire, as he had, was worthy of the utmost trust. It was the beginning of the release of her tightly-controlled feelings; the beginning of their love affair.

A flush passed over her body from the top of her head to the end of her toes. Could the very thought of Lawren Drake in this room and in this bed have such an effect on her even after all these years?

She threw off the covers in an attempt to cool down, but her body was on fire.

Now fully awake, she moved over to the window and

opened the curtains. She felt as if leaning her forehead on the cold window pane would start the process of calming the heat raging in her body.

Looking out to the garden lit by moonlight she saw a shadowy figure advancing to the gate that led to Helen's Hill.

At first her mind could not grasp the sight. Why would Ashley be out at such an hour? Who else could it be? Bev and Alan were not at home. There were no other near neighbours. She watched as intently as her drifting thoughts would allow. The figure seemed to bypass the metal gate and start on the uphill climb then it disappeared. Trying to scan the area for the dim figure was giving her a headache. She thought of returning to the bedside to collect her eyeglasses but she was far too tired and dizzy to contemplate the move.

Perhaps if she just sat down on the velvet chair for a moment, she would feel stronger and then she could go back to sleep once the headache had eased.

Ashley found Anna slumped in the chair, by a dying fire, the next morning.

She saw at once that all was not well and she berated herself for not checking sooner. She had not wished to disturb the sleeper too soon and now she could see what a mistake that was.

Her Aunt Anna was a woman of unusual good health and stamina. She had endured much in her life and triumphed over it all, but this pajama–clad figure hardly resembled the person who had gone to bed the night before. Ashley could see a flush on her cheeks and she was decidedly groggy when she heard Ashley's shocked voice.

"Let's get you back into bed for now. I have a tray ready downstairs and I'll bring it right up here in just a moment." She frantically straightened the bedcovers, noting dampness on the pillow and quickly turning it to the other side, then hauled the limp figure of Anna onto her feet, practically lifting her into the bed. The whole time this was happening the older woman was mumbling something about a stranger in the back garden.

Ashley was appalled. She needed to get help.

She rushed downstairs and fetched the teapot, pouring out a hot cup and adding it to the tray set with a milk jug. She found a sugar bowl and dropped two spoonsful into the tea thinking it was needed. She jogged up the stairs to the master bedroom and through the opened door and found Anna dozing in an upright position. Fearing to disturb her, she set down the tray and stepped outside into the hallway where she could hear without being overheard.

In a moment her cell phone was in her hand and she was phoning her mother, Donna. She could hear the dialling tone before she realized it would be very early in the morning in Canada but she needed to hear her mother's voice and hoped she would not mind being disturbed so early.

"Who's calling?" The voice was sleepy. Her mother could not see without her glasses.

"Mom, it's me!"

"Ashley! What time is this to be calling? Where are you?"

"I'm sorry, Mom. I'm in Scotland with Aunt Anna and I need your advice."

"My advice is to call later. Ricky has to get up for work when it's light and he won't appreciate being wakened so early."

"Listen, Mom, this is important! Aunt Anna is ill and I am here alone. I don't know what to do."

At once Donna sat up in bed. Her daughter was a self-sufficient young woman. This panic in her voice indicated a real problem. She spoke into the phone in a whisper but she was listening.

"What seems to be the trouble?"

"I don't know. She is very hot and disoriented. I found her on a chair instead of in her bed. What should I do?"

"Isn't her friend Bev, nearby? You could call or even walk over."

"That's the trouble. There's no one around to help. I feel so useless."

"Pull yourself together, Ashley! You will have to find the name of the local doctor's office and call them. I think they still do house visits in Scotland. It doesn't sound as if Anna should be moved. Do you suspect a heart attack or a stroke?"

"God! I hope not. Too much time has passed already to get treatment for those."

"Right, then, Ash! Go get on the phone at once. Call me later when you know what's happening. I have to go now, Ricky's stirring."

She ran down the stairs to the kitchen after a quick glance to see if there was any change in Anna's position. Frantically opening all the kitchen drawers looking for a notebook, she suddenly remembered a sheet of paper on the wall of the pantry with local numbers for anyone renting the house.

With trembling fingers she dialled the number for the doctor's surgery in Oban and danced from foot to foot waiting impatiently for an answer.

"Doctors Jansen and Williams' Surgery. How can I help you?"

Sending aloft a prayer of thanks that she had found a person rather than an answering service, Ashley launched into an account of where she was and who she was with.

"Did you say Anna Drake?"

"Yes, and she is quite ill. I need a doctor to come and see her as soon as possible."

"Just a second while I find out if she's a patient registered here."

The second was stretching into a minute while Ashley tried to keep her temper. Didn't they know this was urgent? What if Anna Drake had never before required medical attention in Oban? What would she do then? The nearest large town was Fort William, several miles away.

"Hello? I had to check back in our records before I found Mrs. Drake. She once came here for a prescription some years ago. She is a resident of Canada, I believe, but she owns property here."

"Yes! Yes! Can the doctor come *today*? She's not fit to be moved."

"I'll inform Dr. Jansen. He's on duty today. There are several patients in the waiting room but I think he should be with you around the noon hour."

"Thank you! What should I do in the meantime?"

"Keep the patient warm and quiet and watch for any signs of distress."

Ashley put her phone back in her pocket and rubbed her hands over her face. At least help was on its way. She could breathe again although watching for signs of distress was troublesome. There were plenty of signs already and she had no way of determining which might be significant. Nevertheless she headed back upstairs to check on Anna and watch the clock hands make their plodding way around the dial.

Dr. Edmund Jansen arrived on the doorstep at 12:30pm to find a very nervous young woman waiting.

He had trouble locating the house. It was a twenty minute drive from the town and he was somewhat distracted by the lovely scenery on the way. He had been a locum in Oban for only a few months and opportunities to drive around in the surrounding countryside had not been presented until now.

After he had to reverse back to the laneway leading to the house he drove much faster and left his car at the gate. He could see someone watching out of the large window so he grabbed his bag and stood tall to add presence to his stature. It amazed him how many people were wary of his youth. As if recent medical training would not be superior to that of an aging doctor.

"I'll show you upstairs, Doctor. I am a great-niece of Anna Drake. She arrived here from Canada just yesterday and was taken ill overnight. I can't see any improvement since I called your office this morning."

"Where can I wash my hands?"

"There's a washroom across the hall from her bedroom."

He noticed her use of the word 'washroom' and the accent denoting she, also, was from Canada.

Before he had entered medical training, he had travelled extensively and the east coast of Canada was one of his favourite places. Now was not the time for that conversation, however.

He asked the young woman to stay nearby while he examined his patient. There was no need of a thermometer to determine she had a high fever. She was flushed and had the glazed look of someone

in pain.

"I am Dr. Jansen, Anna. I am going to help make you more comfortable. Tell me how you feel."

"I feel awful. I am hot, my head hurts and my throat hurts too."

He took a tongue depressor out of his bag and looked at her throat. His brain was processing all the possible adult illnesses related to these symptoms and he was arriving at a somewhat unlikely diagnosis.

A quick look at her chest soon confirmed his suspicion. There were raised, red lumps on her chest similar to the ones he had seen inside her throat.

"I think you may have contracted chickenpox, Anna."

It was Ashley who responded with alarm. "Is that possible? I thought it was a childhood disease. Will she need to go to hospital? How serious is it?"

"Well, first of all let's not worry the patient with suppositions. I would say this is an adult onset of the disease which can happen even if a person had it as a child. The question is; where was your aunt exposed to another virulent dose of the virus? I understand she was recently on an airplane."

"Surely no one would go on a flight with a communicable disease?"

Ashley was hearing her tone of voice become more strident with her concern. *Was this young doctor qualified to diagnose? Chickenpox? Really? How likely was that?*

"It can take several days before the symptoms are displayed. Your aunt, or anyone else, would not necessarily know if a person was already infectious."

Ashley bit her lip and tried to remember if she had had chickenpox as a child. It did not guarantee immunity in this situation but she was young and presumably more resistant. In any case she was here and she would not leave Anna alone in this state.

A strained voice entered her thoughts. They had been talking over the patient's head and the patient had information to convey, despite her difficulty in talking.

"Doctor, I held a child who might have been sick while I was on the plane. Evie was very hot and restless."

He turned at once to Anna. "It could be the answer. If I am right you will be quite uncomfortable for several days. I will give you a prescription to help reduce the fever and ward off some of the itching that will come. As long as you have someone here with you we can keep you at home for now, but I will be checking up on you in a day or so."

With that, he jumped up and signalled to Ashley to follow him. When they reached the kitchen he said,

"She will be inclined to scratch and that must be resisted. Buy some calamine lotion at the chemist. It's an old remedy but patients find it helpful although it makes a pink mess of clothing. She will need lots to drink but as her throat will become coated in blisters she will find it difficult to drink or eat. If you have straws around, those will make it easier. Call the surgery if you have serious concerns. Just try to wait it out until she feels a bit better."

Before Ashley could ask any questions, he took a look around the kitchen then crossed the entrance hall into the lounge next door. She followed, wondering what he was doing. This was no time for a house tour.

"Is there sleeping accommodation in this large room? It would be easier for you if your patient could be downstairs. I passed a small toilet on my way in. She won't want a bath for a few days so that will be handy for now. Don't rush her until she feels up to walking downstairs."

There was a lot of information for Ashley to process but she summoned up the necessary response while the doctor's dark gaze was upon her.

"Um, yes, this couch is a pull-out bed. It's quite comfy. I've slept in it myself and there's a fireplace here for additional warmth. Thank you, Dr. Jansen."

She felt guilty for being so abrupt earlier but he had not seemed to notice. His head was down as he scribbled a prescription and put it in her hand.

"I'll be back in a day or two, Miss… ? I take it you are staying here?"

"Oh, call me Ashley. Ashley Stanton. I am staying here with my great-aunt for several weeks."

"Good. She'll be glad of your help. You are somewhat isolated here."

With that he was gone, marching down the gravel path as if he had an urgent appointment somewhere.

Fast and efficient. He doesn't waste any time.

Ashley sighed, closed the door, and ran over in her mind all the necessary requirements to keep Anna comfortable. The immediate thing that arose was the need to call on Cameron to take her into Oban to fetch supplies and get the prescription filled. But first she would check on the invalid. It looked as if she was about to get a crash course in nursing for elderly patients. Just as well she loved the patient as she did. It was not going to be easy.

Chapter Five

❧

It took two more days before Anna Drake was steady enough on her feet to walk downstairs, leaning on Ashley's arm. The fever had persisted and it was increasingly difficult for her to get a comfortable place to lie on the bed. The red blisters had now emerged on her waistline and on her chest. Ashley had dug around in the storage closet and found two long, cotton nightshirts that could slip over Anna's head without the elastic from pajamas irritating her spots. The calamine lotion was cooling and soothing but between sweat and pink stains, Ashley had to wash a nightgown each day and iron it dry. The bedding went into the small washing machine in the larder a sheet at a time, then hung outside to dry in the breeze that had replaced the wet weather.

There was a great deal of running up and down and taking drinks upstairs while trying to coax her aunt to eat something. The doctor had been right about the lounge bed being an easier location.

However, there was something the doctor did not know. While Anna was drifting in and out of consciousness, she was talking in a very low voice.

Ashley heard the murmur from across the hall where her own bedroom door had been left open.

She tiptoed in to make sure all was well and was struck immediately by the rambling story that filled the quiet, dark room with dramatic events. It sounded like an incident from Anna's life in the house.

She was faced with a moral dilemma. Should be listening? It could be very private memories unlocked by the fever.

On the other hand, she was beginning to notice a cohesive line of thought. This might well be vital material for the book or article she was here to write. Could she afford to ignore the opportunity?

The decision was made quickly. Ashley returned to her bedroom, fetched a notebook and pen, grabbed a dressing gown from the wardrobe, and settled quietly on the velvet chair by the fireside.

She stifled her conscience by fervently promising to ask permission of Anna Mason Drake before using any part of what she was hearing.

By the glow of the fire she began to write.

Are you there?
Always.
I was sick once before in this house. I thought my mother had come to nurse me but that was long, long ago. I feel bad now. It's better when you are near.
Always.
Do you remember, my darling?
I remember everything.
The Rings? Do you remember when you gave me the ring?
You wore it every day after that.
I wear it still. It is a symbol of our love.
You wouldn't let me buy you a wedding ring.
Of course not. What could surpass a soulmate pledge?

Our wedding was perfect. Just we two and a parson in a sacred Abbey overlooking the sea.
Perfect.
We danced.
I don't remember the music.
You hummed a tune in my ear.
You kissed my hand.
We lay in bed listening to the waves break on the shore.
We talked all night.
Most of the night.
Most of the night.
I think I will sleep now.
Sleep well, my darling.
Will you be there?
Always.

Ashley Stanton was an accomplished journalist. She took the fevered ramblings and devised the missing parts of the conversation Anna Drake was clearly having with her late husband. Some words were very clear. She had enough perception to realize she was quite possibly inventing responses but the situation seemed to warrant it.

The room was darkened; lit only by the dying embers of the fire. It was the strangest experience she had ever encountered. The hair on the back of Ashley's neck stood up when Anna began to speak.

Her aunt's voice was feeble but, even so, the emotions came through. Ashley could tell when there was humour or sadness. Overall, the feeling was as if two dear friends were talking over old times together in the dark.

She could not see anything other than the hump of a shoulder under the bedclothes but she had the definite sensation of a third person in the room. The thought of a ghost occurred. It was unthinkable.

Ghosts were for dark, ancient times and foreign places, not this bright and airy home surrounded by beauty and love.

And so, love must be the key.

The love between Anna and Lawren was something she had seen with her own eyes.

It was real. It was true.

If that love in some way survived his death, would it be so impossible to believe?

She was beginning to think not. She had been eavesdropping on a very private moment, occasioned by illness perhaps, but nonetheless real. She had been the unwitting observer of a strange and mystical experience.

As a journalist who wished to tell their love story, she could not ignore the opportunity presented to her.

※

In the morning, Anna was still fevered but somehow, she felt better. Had she dreamed? She could not remember anything specific. Her throat still hurt when she swallowed although the thought of some warm, light broth had an appeal that had been missing for some days.

When Ashley arrived to open the drapes and scrape out the ashes of the fire, she noticed signs of improvement and hastened to make tea, heat soup and prepare the patient for the doctor's visit.

She said nothing of the night's events.

Edmund Jansen found himself eager to return to the McCaig Estate house. In the few days since his first visit, he had enquired of the senior doctor if he knew anything of the inhabitants.

During lunch, consisting of sandwiches and mineral water consumed at Connor Williams' desk, Edmund's question was given due consideration between thoughtful munching and frequent wiping of the doctor's heavy grey mustache.

"Well, laddie, despite my age, I don't go back as far as the original family although you may find their history in the Oban Library.

I mind plenty gossip about Miss Helen Dunlop, however. Now, then, she's the previous occupant, supposed to be some relative of the current lady, Anna Drake.

Are you keeping up, Ed?"

"I believe so. You said the Dunlop person was supposed to be a relative?"

"Aye. There's a wee bit of a mystery there. Some in the town think they know more than me but most are saying little about it."

Edmund had hoped for a simple answer to his enquiry. Now he recognized the old, sing-song tone of a Gaelic storyteller in full mode. There was no stopping Connor Williams at this juncture. Edmund sat back with drink in hand, a surreptitious glance at his watch revealing a full thirty minutes before his next appointment.

Connor continued.

"So, Helen Dunlop arrived in town without any fanfare. The only one who knew a thing about it was George McLennan the solicitor, and he was keeping his cards close to his chest. It was his wife, that Canadian woman Jeanette, who let slip the McCaig property was bought outright. *With cash*."

Edmund's mind was drifting already but he knew the significance of the last statement. Few houses in Scotland were purchased this way, prices being what they were. He was currently renting a small room

and looked forward to the far distant time when he could afford a dwelling he could call his own.

"When I said Helen Dunlop arrived in town, that was not quite accurate. She never showed her face in Oban at all. She lived out in the country like a hermit, most nearly. It was years before her actual presence was known and even then it was her actions that drew the town's attentions."

"What did she do? Strip off all her clothes and run around McCaig's Folly singing madly?"

Connor Williams put aside his glass of water and lowered his beetling eyebrows until his gaze was centred on his colleague.

"Ah wouldna be making jokes like that laddie. Folks around here are verra proud of our town's landmark and, by the way, proud of Helen Dunlop herself who did a number of good things for the town before she died. Have a wee bit respect for your elders and betters."

Edmund was duly admonished. Doc Williams remarks were intended to be a caution. He sat up straight and summoned more attention to what was developing into a long tale.

When would it get to the part about that Ashley girl?

"So, as I was saying how Helen Dunlop made her mark. First of all she set about improving the old estate house. She had local workers mend the chimneys and repair the drystone walls. The men brought back stories about the handsome older lady with generous ways who cared about her property and asked sensible questions that showed a deep interest in the community. It was known she employed a local taxi driver to take her to George McLennan's office and she was always dressed smartly on those occasions. George wouldn't reveal much about his client but the detective he employed made enquiries in Glasgow and Canada and those phone calls went through George's secretary for payment."

"Wait a minute! How did a detective get into this?"

"Are you sleeping again, Ed? Did I not say how Mistress Dunlop was looking for lost family members?

Well, to cut a long story short, since your attention span is ridiculously brief my boy, the missing relative turned out to be Anna Mason."

"I thought she was Anna *Drake*. That's the name I was given."

Connor clicked his tongue several times in annoyance. "The lady is Anna Drake *now,* and I can only hope you recognize her surname. She was married to the famous artist

Lawren Drake, of course. Now don't you even start on asking about the Mason/Dunlop connection. If you are so curious about it, you can ask for yourself.

Are you not booked to see a patient this afternoon? Get a move on, Laddie!"

Edmund's mouth opened and closed, somewhat like a fish. There was no useful purpose served by stating Dr. William's long tale had prevented him from leaving.

He cleaned up the remains of his lunch and beat a quick retreat.

Chapter Six

When the young woman answered his knock, Edmund immediately noticed her fair hair. On his previous visit it had been twisted up at the back of her head but now it was framing her face and falling below her shoulders in soft waves.

Touchable, he thought, before his professional training asserted itself.

"How is our patient today, Miss err…. Stanton?"

"Ashley. Please call me Ashley."

Well, that was painfully obvious! Grow up and get on with the business.

He busied himself with his medical bag to hide his embarrassment. Ashley went ahead into the bright kitchen and signalled for him to follow.

"I wanted a word with you doctor, before you see Anna. She's downstairs now as you suggested and that is much easier for both of us. She's still feverish off and on even with the medicine you prescribed. The calamine helps with the itching but there seem to be more spots.

How long will this last?"

"She'll be over the worst in two weeks or so. Try to keep

her comfortable. It's always harder on adults, as I said before. I will take a look, if that's all right?"

"Please do. She's awake. It's wonderful of you to make house calls. This doesn't happen in Canada, I can assure you. May I offer you tea or coffee?"

"Tea would be great, thank you."

He probably shouldn't accept the offer but Ashley had given him a conversational opening and he wanted to take it.

Anna was sitting up against the pillows Ashley had piled at her back. She was wearing one of the voluminous, white cotton nightshirts that buttoned from the neck down.

Most of her energy lately had been diverted to the task of resisting the itch on each and every lump, bump and blister on her skin. The original ones on her chest and face were drying up at last but Ashley had looked online and warned her sternly not to scratch as the scabs would come off leaving a scar behind.

The anti-itch treatment regimen they had devised together consisted of application of pink calamine lotion which cooled the itch nicely until it dried. After that, Ashley brought cold water from the fridge and facecloths to be dipped into the bowl then wrung out and dabbed onto the worst areas for further temporary relief.

This process left messy pink streaks on the nightshirt and meant a trip to the nearby washroom where Anna had a wash down in a sink of warm water after which, she usually managed a nap until the entire cycle began again.

When the pleasant young doctor arrived, Anna was waking from the most recent nap and felt pleased she was both clean and dry for his visit.

"Hello, Mrs. Drake. How are you feeling? I see your face is looking better. What about your throat?

I'll take a quick look, if I may?"

Anna opened her mouth for a dry tongue depressor which was removed just before it made her cough.

"Those will be the most bothersome, I suspect."

"Yes, it still hurts to swallow." Her whisper proved how difficult it must be to talk.

"That's not surprising. Your throat is coated with pustules. Keep drinking any liquids you can tolerate and don't worry about solid foods for now. Jelly works for some patients, particularly the little ones.

The fever should diminish soon. It's good that you are close to the downstairs lavatory. A little walking is helpful if you feel up to it."

"I do need to get up for the washroom. I see a bit of improvement daily."

It was about as much as she could manage to say and her voice cracked on the last words.

"Good! I'll ask your nurse to bring in some tea for you before I go."

Anna nodded her thanks and sank down again into the bed.

Ashley was pouring tea from a large, round brown betty teapot into china cups. She immediately took a cup and saucer into Anna and invited the doctor to help himself to sugar, milk, and a plate of what looked like macaroons.

The whole set up reminded Edmund so much of his mother's kitchen in the little east coast fishing village of Rosehearty that it brought a lump to his throat. Seldom nowadays were the times someone poured tea for him. He thought it might be a good idea to plan a quick trip back home again before the weather turned.

At this particular moment, however, he felt relaxed for the first time in ages.

It was just then when the phone began to ring. He jumped

up and spilled his tea into the saucer while reaching for his mobile phone.

Ashley rushed into the kitchen and bumped into him on her way to the handset now jangling every nerve he had.

"It's ours! Sorry, please sit. I'll be just a minute."

It felt awkward listening in as Ashley answered what sounded like a series of questions about her aunt. He tried not to listen but, obviously, she was going to be involved for some time.

No chance for a cozy chat then!

He slipped out before she noticed and was half-way to his car still hearing her voice.

"I know, and I apologize, Jeanette. It's been all go since Anna arrived. She needs constant nursing and I have been so busy. I didn't think anyone knew we were here so no one could be worried."

"Well, my dear, you can expect lot of worried friends on the phone now the word is out. Cameron told his dad you were here and he was sent to collect prescriptions for Anna.

Chickenpox? Unbelievable! Poor Anna, and poor you, Ashley. You are going to be continuing in isolation I'm afraid. I can't risk my two getting it again with our move to the bigger house coming so soon. Fiona is only days from giving birth to her third. I guess it's good luck you were here at all. I don't know how we would have coped with Bev and Alan in the States.

It's bad timing, but good that you have Doc. Jansen on the case. Old Doc Williams is getting a bit past it, I think.

Keep in touch, Ashley. I presume you have already had the pox?"

With that, Jeanette was gone to spread the news.

Ashley turned around and discovered Dr. Jansen had left without a word and without drinking his tea. She rinsed his cup and saucer in the sink then took a breath, twisted back her hair with an elastic band she kept on her wrist when not in use, and slipped back into the darkened lounge, now the bedroom where Anna was fast asleep again.

She inspected her patient them dropped down into a fireside chair. She took a notebook and pen from the table realising it might not be needed. It was not every time Anna slept that she also spoke aloud. It seemed to require a particular type of deep sleep to produce the effect.

This afternoon, Ashley was in luck. The same disembodied voice floated upward.

Are you there?
Always. Are you feeling better?
A little better now.
Good.
Tell me a story. I love your stories.
You know all my stories.
Tell me anyway. Tell me how you learned to paint.
I loved colours. On our street in London, Ontario, there was a house with a big garden.
The owner worked in his garden spring through fall and he didn't object to a kid staring over the wall at all the plants. I would go home and try to draw the flowers using my crayons.
I took the broken pieces and mixed them together to make the tints and shades I needed. I melted the wax together with a match on an old plate I found in the garbage. At school I drew only with pencil. Colours were for my private time.
When did you know you had a special talent?
My father wanted me to be an artist like Lawren Harris, the famous Canadian. He sent me to lessons. I hated the teacher. She told me I was no good and I believed her. So I continued to draw and paint when I was alone. It made me happy. That was what was important to me.
You made many others happy with your work, my darling.

And you too?
Especially me. Will you stay with me always?
Always.

Ashley could recall some of the stories of Lawren's early years with Anna so it was not difficult for her to fill in the blanks.

She made quick notes which she could expand later. For now, there was another load of washing to do. A brisk breeze had sprung up. It would be a good drying day. Later she would make custard and jelly for Anna.

The moment to discuss the private conversations she had overheard could safely be delayed until Great-Aunt Anna had fully recovered.

Chapter Seven

"Ashley, it's Fiona. Jeanette called me. I am so annoyed that I can't be with you to give a helping hand. How is Anna doing?"

"She's coming along. She's a little better each day, I believe. Dr. Jansen is advising me about meds and diet but she's not up to talking on the phone as yet. She'll be so glad to hear you called, Fiona.

May I tell her how *you* are feeling?"

"Oh, I am eager for the new baby to arrive. It won't be long now. Tell Anna the house is almost finished. I am so happy she will be here in Oban to meet the new baby in our new home. Lots of new things arriving!"

"It sounds like it! I'll pass on the news. I know she would ask me to tell you to be careful, if you don't mind me saying it?"

"Ha! I don't mind one little bit, Ashley. I think of Anna Mason Drake as my heaven-sent mother, you know.

Oh dear! I can hear the school bus arriving with the children so I'll say goodbye for now. I am hoping to see you and Anna as soon as she is well enough.

Bye for now!"

Ashley put down the phone and looked at the kitchen wall clock. *4:30pm already!*

The day had flown and she had done nothing to advance her writing project. If she sat down at once and focussed, perhaps she could work on a provisional outline before supper.

Is it a biography or a memoir?

Is it all Anna, or some of my memories as well?

Dare I include the fever dreams?

Is it about Lawren Drake or Anna and Lawren?

Is it to be set in this house?

The last question seemed to be the only one to which she had an answer. Something about being here in Oban where the couple was so happy had the ring of authenticity. It might be possible to write an article based on the estate house events and then, if approved by her publisher, it could be extended to include other locations relating to Lawren's life as an artist.

She began to scribble down ideas. All the paintings in this house would have to be referenced as well as any others in Oban itself. Didn't she hear about a family portrait the artist had done for the McLennan family? And was there not a painting in the local Library gifted by Lawren or Anna? What others might there be in the area? She must ask Anna about that as soon as she was well enough.

A sense of excitement was growing in Ashley despite her tiredness. From previous experience she knew this feeling was the precursor to good writing material. Without the excitement, nothing other people would want to read was possible.

Perhaps the isolation Jeanette had predicted would be beneficial for the writing she had to do. She could at least form the basis of the work and fill in the detail when Anna was able to participate.

For now, she must make sure Anna recovered in full spirits. So many in Oban were looking forward to seeing her fit and well. She was glad the doctor was supervising. Nursing was not Ashley's strong point.

She hoped she was doing everything that was required. Anna was a precious person but she was not young any more. The responsibility weighed on Ashley. If, God forbid, Anna did not recover well, the blame was sure to fall on the shoulders of her caregiver.

With this dire prediction in mind, Ashley set aside her laptop and went to make custard and jelly to tempt her patient's appetite. It was increasingly clear to her how much depended on Anna Drake's recovery.

Anna awakened with a slight headache, aching eyes and the usual itching all over her skin. From this, she knew it must be time for a re-application of the calamine. She was getting impatient with the amount of time it was taking for her to feel well enough to begin to do everything for herself. Ashley was doing a wonderful job of nursing but it was not what she had come to Oban to do. That task was one that Anna had committed to although they had not had any real discussion about the shape and content of her story about Lawren. Real discussions would have to wait until she could speak more than four words without pain in her throat.

She took a moment to think about the highlights of their life together. Their courtship, if you could call it by such an old-fashioned term, was not what most people would call normal. When she thought back to those days, everything circled around Helen's portrait. Anna's desire to find an artist to do the work was the reason she met Lawren in the first place, and the reason she established a connection to him.

After she had seen his work on her visit to his studio, she knew he was special but it took too long until she saw him as a potential life partner. In all the slow progress toward that realization, it was Lawren who made the moves. She was stuck in the fear of public humiliation when others realized he was younger. Now she could laugh at herself for this. No one cared. No one who counted had ever made any remarks along those lines. In fact, it was Jeanette who declared every woman should have a partner younger than she was. It was generally supposed to mean a woman would survive longer and if she wanted a companion in old age the chances were better if her male partner was a few years younger.

Sadly, this had not happened in their case. Lawren's unexpected death had left Anna alone and bereft for the second time in her life. The benefit in tackling this dreadful circumstance as a mature woman, was the self-confidence she had acquired along the way. Her Samba Plus friends, (Jeanette and Fiona were additions to the original group) had always been by her side and they were still. Her experiences in Scotland and with the A Plus Knitwear business, had given her finances and property as well as appreciation for all the good things in her life. It would have been a disgrace to collapse and bemoan her fate after the wonders of each minute she had shared with her husband.

Although many of her friends thought they knew about the secret marriage, they were wrong; just as wrong as they were about Lawren's sudden death. She had concealed much about these two crucial events. They were deeply private.

Was it now time to reveal the real stories to the world? Time to set the record straight?

She had committed to Ashley's writing idea. She could not imagine anyone more sympathetic to their love story. This illness had forced Anna to face the reality of her eventual decline into old age and, God forbid, possible mental disintegration. If she chose not to take this opportunity, the story behind the headlines would remain untold. Is that what she wanted?

The dire warning of the legacy of untold secrets was exemplified in her own family story. Her mother and father had fled Scotland for Canada, hoping to leave betrayals and mistakes in their wake, but the results had been disastrous. A forgotten daughter abandoned in the past; a marriage of sins unforgiven; a family ripped asunder and never to be repaired; a brother who would be an adult before he learned of his mother's secret older son. The more she thought of it, the more Anna saw waves of pain and shame and regret and sorrow washing back and forth in the wake of bad decisions and hardened hearts.

The McLeods had been victims of all this. Only Helen Dunlop had been able to rise above the life fate had decreed for her. She, alone, had turned evil into good and in doing so had passed on to her female relative the torch of truth. Anna could not let the torch be extinguished. Lawren would say the opportunity to set the record straight was now before her. It was her duty. His Drake family had also suffered from hard-hearted decisions that split them apart and separated one branch from another.

Anna knew she lacked the ability to write this story but she had at her disposal a person who could write, record, and untangle the strands, starting from her grandmother's early life and moving into the present.

Anna and Lawren's story was a part of that, of course, and because of his fame, it would be the part that would draw the attention of a publisher. It was essential that Anna's message about transparency and truth be clear from the start, or the book would lose its focus and become just another celebrity exposé.

She pushed up against the pillows with the sense of an important decision made. Now she must get well so the process could begin. There would be weeks of talk ahead and she needed to be clear of mind and voice to tackle the hours required for the task.

At this thought, she considered an alternative. She could summarize Lawren's family story for him as his father had passed away years ago and the only remaining relative she knew of, had gone to Australia decades before without leaving any contact information. But, her half-brother, Philip, could tell the story of his side of the family with the Purdy/McLeod link and perhaps her new-found McLeod clan in Glasgow might add their discoveries. What had started as a simple story of a love affair had now become a saga stretching across generations and bridging seas, but with the same theme of damaging secrets and forgiveness withheld.

It was a huge task. It remained to be seen if Ashley was willing to undertake such an epic, also, whether other family members could be persuade to participate. A sense of urgency compelled Anna to slide over to the edge of the bed and stand up. She needed to get her ideas down on paper since she was not yet capable of speaking for the length of time it would take for her to convey her thoughts to Ashley.

She staggered over to the little table beside the fireside armchair where she could see a notebook lying waiting with pen on top.

Surely, Ashley would not object to losing a page or so?

She plopped down onto the chair and picked up the notebook. Ashley had been writing something. There were several pages of brief notes and Anna had to flip through them to find a blank page to pull out for her own ideas.

Suddenly the words on the close–written pages caught her eye. The word 'always' recurred several times. What was this? It read like a kind of dream sequence but parts of it were familiar as if Ashley had overheard something Anna might have said. By now she could not resist reading all of it. The fear of invading her niece's privacy arrived and disappeared almost simultaneously. She felt impelled to find out what this writing could mean. She turned on the lamp on the table to focus her eyes better and wiped them with the sleeve of her nightdress. The sudden movement pushed the lamp to the side and it fell onto the carpet with a thump and a flash as the light bulb smashed on impact and the meagre light extinguished.

Anna cried out, immediately regretting her impulse as her throat stabbed with pain.

Ashley heard both the cry and the crash and ran in from the kitchen with her heart in her mouth.

What now?

She found Anna shaking and tearful, a broken lamp shedding particles of glass on the carpet and her notebook lying open in Anna's lap.

Ashley immediately guessed what had happened and she felt anguish at what her aunt might deduce from the notebook writing.

This is not the way I wanted to introduce the subject of her dream conversations!

Her first priority was to make sure Anna was all right. It was clear from the state of her nightdress that a change of clothing was necessary. Ashley had a fresh nightdress airing in the kitchen over the handle of the Aga, but she thought Anna would be ready for a warm, soothing bath. She helped her patient over to the bed murmuring reassurances that everything would be fine in a few minutes. Then she ran upstairs to fill the bath with water and an oatmeal-based product the doctor had advised. All the while she was watching the bath fill and testing the temperature, she was keenly aware that she was avoiding the difficult conversation that must come. She had no idea how to explain to Anna what she had read on the notebook pages but for the moment she cast that aside. If Anna could manage to climb the stairs and settle into the bath, Ashley could change the bed and sort out the damaged lamp and try to think.

It was the mental space she needed. It did not look like Anna Drake was in any fit state to question her at length, so she had time to concoct a reasonable explanation, if one existed.

Her heart was thumping wildly. It was possible she had

broken faith with Anna and the entire book idea would be dismissed. This was bad, but even worse was the thought that Anna would see her as having betrayed her confidence and the special relationship they had always shared would be gone like the morning mist.

Anna welcomed the bath idea. She leaned heavily on Ashley as they climbed the stairs and she sank into the warm water with a sigh of relief. The steamy air in the washroom was kind to her ravaged throat and Ashley had turned on the wall heater so the atmosphere outside the bath would not shock her patient with cold air when she emerged.

Anna relaxed and slid down beneath the water for a moment so her head, which was also covered in irritating spots, could feel the benefit of the moisturizing oatmeal. Despite the shock she had experienced downstairs, she decided to wait until she could speak comfortably before challenging Ashley. If she knew the girl, it was likely she would offer an explanation soon enough.

There was a great deal to discuss on both sides.

For now, Anna was relishing the skin comfort she was presently enjoying. It might be the bath, or it might be the mental effort she had expended on the future plan for the book project, but she was beginning to feel as if the long days and nights of illness were finally behind her.

Chapter Eight

It took three more days of hot drinks and nourishing soups before Anna's throat repaired enough for her to be able to speak for any length of time without discomfort.

Ashley, as expected, had offered her apology for the shock Anna had experienced on reading her notes. Somehow, Anna accepted the notion that she had spoken to Lawren in her fevered dreams. Ashley wondered if it had happened before this, but she was reluctant to broach the subject. She was just relieved that her aunt had not been horrified at the intrusion into her private mind.

They put the whole incident aside and concentrated on getting Anna back onto her feet, literally as well as metaphorically.

So much time in bed had resulted in weakened muscles. Anna needed a walking stick to take the weight off her back which was painful if she stood upright for longer than ten minutes at a time but she was able to wear her usual pajamas and sit in the kitchen for a while and she preferred to sleep once again in the double bed upstairs. Daily baths were the most beneficial thing she had discovered although Ashley was concerned about slipping in the bathroom and had found a chair which she padded with towels and positioned beside the bath so Anna could pull herself out of the water more easily and sit there while she dried herself.

Doctor Jansen approve of all these measures when he visited.

"Our patient is progressing well," he stated, while Ashley tried once more to provide him with a cup of tea.

"However, I must say the nurse looks as if she needs a bit of a break."

"What?" Ashley was just catching up with the conversation while calculating if she had enough milk left to fill the jug. It was time for another order of groceries now that Anna could eat some solid food.

"I mean, this has been a difficult period for you, Ashley. You should take the chance to get some fresh air and a change of scene."

"Oh, I get plenty of air when I am hanging out the washing and carting out buckets of ash from the fireplaces, but I guess I do need to restock the larder."

He cleared his throat. This was not going the way he had intended. It was a risk to try a different tactic but another house call was not likely to be required and this could be his last chance.

"Well, if Mrs. Drake agrees, I could take you into Oban this afternoon and you could shop there."

Ashley put down the milk jug and looked at Edmund Jansen with new eyes. This was an uncommonly kind offer. She considered whether Scottish doctors usually included this type of service with their home visits then discounted the thought as highly unlikely. So, the offer must be more personal than professional.

Aha!

"Dr. Jansen, that would be most helpful. Please finish your tea and I'll check with my aunt to see what she needs. If she agrees, I will be ready in a flash. I don't want to delay you."

With that, she was off upstairs to talk to Anna who was sitting by the fireside with a book.

"I think it's a splendid idea, Ash. You go. I'll be fine here. I'll do some phone calls. Oh, if you can find me a long cashmere sweater, I would love that. My skin is still very tender and it needs some TLC."

"Certainly! I'll see what I can get in town. I won't be long. I'll take my phone with me in case you feel worse. Could you alert Cameron for me? If he's not available later I will just take a taxi from the grocery store. Thank you!"

Anna noticed how eager Ashley was to get away for a spell and she could not blame the girl. She had been shut up in the house for weeks with a non-communicative invalid. Not much fun for a young woman.

Ashley stopped for a minute in her bedroom adjoining the washroom. She combed through her hair and swiped some pink lipstick on her lips. There wasn't time for more. Her outdoor coat was downstairs with her purse and credit card.

She raced down the stairs like a kid let out of school. Just like a kid, she felt excited. The question was whether it was the taste of freedom causing the excitement, or the person who was supplying the freedom? For the moment she did not stop to search for the answer.

Edmund Jansen was standing waiting at the front door. He helped her into her coat and made sure she had the house key and without any further discussion, they were off down the gravel path and roaring back to Oban.

Anna thought how different the house felt when she was the only occupant. A silence fell in which she could hear the sound of birds. A woodpecker must be in the fir trees that marked the western border of the property. Wind soughed in the chimney and a gust threatened to extinguish the peat flames.

These sounds had been missing for some time. Her ears had been blocked during the worst of the fever and now, each tiny outdoor reminder was all the more welcome.

The season had changed since she had first arrived. The long, bright days of autumn were fading fast. Already the drapes were being drawn earlier in the evening and storms from the sea could be expected soon. It was the lovely, cozy period of retreating indoors and appreciating home comforts. And yet, she felt she had been confined indoors for too long and the charms of her country home had been lost to her. The coming months were bound to be busy if the writing project were to proceed but there were also other priorities to be attended to.

When this happy thought occurred, Anna rose up and went to the bedside phone.

"Jeanette? Is this a good time to call?"

"Anna! Thank God! I was beginning to think I'd never hear that sweet voice again. How are you feeling my dear?"

"I am returning to life, I believe. My throat is better each day hence this call. Please give me the latest on everyone. Ashley has passed on the news, of course, but I feel so out of touch."

"Bless that Ashley! If she hadn't been on the scene, you would have been dragged off to hospital somewhere. Everyone has been calling me to avoid disturbing you. I am the point person, at the moment, so I am well supplied for this situation. Sit back and I'll fill you in."

Anna had to smile. Jeanette had a certain Canadian style. She did not 'beat around the bush', as they said in these parts. Anna knew she would be saved from having to ask any further questions. She settled down against the bed pillows and relaxed.

"So, we McLennans are ready for the move to the bigger house. All the redecorating has been done. The children have sorted out their toys and I have made strenuous efforts to clear out every cupboard and storage bin. You know how I hate clutter. I mean to start off with everything tidy and in its appointed place. Even George has helped, after I threatened to take his assigned office in the new house and turn it into something more useful unless he got his files, his mail and his messages in proper order."

Anna laughed. Jeanette was a force to be reckoned with. She considered asking if there were to be some of her antique finds added to the décor but that was another topic for another day.

"As for the Campbell establishment: George and I went over there a couple of days ago and, Anna, you will have to see what they have built. It's in the most beautiful location, of course. They had the pick of the estate but what's so amazing is the way they chose to build. Fiona was determined to have an environmentally sound project and the whole place is green from top to bottom. I won't say more. It needs to be seen by your own eyes.

The best news from Gordon is that Fiona has finally gone into hospital. The third Campbell of the clan is arriving imminently. I'll call you as soon as I hear.

Oh, I believe Bev and Alan are due home in a day or so. Bev forced me to tell her about your illness and she is determined to see you as soon as they reach Oban. She says wild horses won't keep her away and she has had chickenpox as well as the shingles vaccination so she is safe.

I think that's all for now. So good to be back in touch, Anna! We'll have quite the reunion as soon as you are well enough to withstand all the hugs and kisses heading your way."

"Oh, Jeanette! This is the best medicine possible. I feel so much better already with all this to look forward to."

Jeanette noted a catch in Anna's voice. *The poor darling has had a terrible time but it will be over soon now. Just as well I decided not to tell Alina how bad Anna has been. All she knows about is a bad throat infection. She would have been rushing across the Atlantic on the first plane if I hadn't said how well Ashley has been handling things.*

"Right, then! Be good, and do what the doctor says. Give yourself a hug. Bye for now."

Anna fought between laughter and tears. It was so good to know she had not been forgotten. This call had been the perfect way for her to focus on the future and put the last few weeks behind her as the bad memory it had been.

Fiona's baby and Bev's arrival. This was, truly, cause for celebration.

She decided to have a wash and get dressed then go downstairs to start supper for Ashley when she returned from town. There was a new strength in her step and a song in her heart.

Ashley spent part of the trip in Dr. Jansen's car taking quick, sidelong glances at his face. She had not previously seen him as anything other than a busy professional who had met her needs, but now she had the chance to see him as a man. And an attractive man at that.

She gave herself a mental shake. Had the past weeks affected her so much that she had not noticed him as a male person? Certainly, he was a good doctor. That was obvious. Had she thrown a veil of unobtainability over him because of his profession? In any case it was time to start all over with Edmund Jansen. He had given her an opening and she would be an idiot not to take advantage of that.

Now that she was aware of him in this totally new way, she began to note the details. He had the dark good looks of a Northern Scot. She had heard Fiona describe such looks as Border Black Douglas's.

She had no idea where he came from but his dark hair and almost black eyes in a pale face which was marked by the shadow of his beard, fit the description.

He wore an overcoat of a standard type, useful in rain or

wind, with the collar pulled up to hide the length of his hair. A tie peeked out from his suit jacket and it was a surprisingly bright, green patterned, version with a tight knot.

Not entirely locked down into the medical mode, then. There could be possibilities there.

She turned away to watch the scenery roll past and wondered what his choice of casual wear would reveal. Closely following on this thought was one where she speculated on the possibility of ever seeing him in more casual attire. At this, she cleared her throat and leaned her forehead on the cool glass pane.

"Did you say something, Ashley?"

The way he said her name was suddenly quite intimate. It was probably just the hint of an accent but it sounded different.

"What? No, I was watching the clouds rolling by. Do you think it will rain soon? I haven't been here long enough to read the weather like most Scots seem to be able to do."

"I'm in the same boat, to some degree. My family is from the east coast. I can read the signs of a North Sea storm approaching with no trouble at all but the west coast with its Atlantic winds is another matter altogether."

"Does that mean you haven't been in these parts for very long?"

She knew she was fishing for information but men don't usually give out much without a prompt.

"I've been here for four months now and I've been kept so busy at the surgery it's a wonder I found my way to the farmhouse. Do you live there permanently with your aunt?"

"Oh, no! She's my great-aunt but I live with the rest of my family in Canada on Prince Edward Island.

I have been in Oban several times over the years. It's a lovely area. It's a pity you haven't had a chance to see more of it. Don't you get a day off here and there?"

She knew, if he was not totally stupid, this was an invitation.

"The problem is, Ashley, I'm usually on call even in my off time. Dr. Williams can't manage the late hours nowadays, so it's difficult to plan anything adventurous."

She jumped in with both feet.

"Would you be at all interested in visiting a nearby castle?"

The car sped up briefly. Ashley presumed excitement had affected his driving foot.

"That sounds amazing! If it's not too far away, I could possibly return quickly if there was an emergency call. Could you arrange such a visit?"

"Just let me know your next free day, and we'll see what can be done. You can't be allowed to live here and not enjoy the local sights."

Got him! I'll call Gordon and put him on alert. I've been at Glenmorie often enough to do the tour on my own if Gordon is busy.

A comfortable silence now descended on the occupants of the doctor's car. There were smiles on faces that had not been evident before and Ashley Stanton had something new and personal to look forward to besides housework and worry about the book.

Chapter Nine

Bev Matthews was anxious to return home and she knew Alan felt the same. They had been in the States for over a month and despite enjoying amazing hospitality from Eric's friends, it was time to get back to 'real' life in the farmhouse among the Scottish hills.

Eric's presentation of new technologies for computer systems had gone off very well although neither of his parents understood more than a word or two. The most exciting part of their stay had been when James and Caroline arrived unexpectedly from Brussels to join in the family celebration. It was so reassuring for Bev to see her sons together again and to know, despite the distances between them and the differences in their career paths, they were still the same responsible, capable boys she had brought up on her own in Canada, then moved to live in Scotland with Alan after they married. The bond between them had never changed.

Now Caroline blended into the mix almost seamlessly. She had a good sense of humour which she claimed was the only way to survive having grown up with a techie brother. She and Eric hit it off immediately and their conversation showed how advanced European communications had become.

The two spoke together earnestly for hours and Caroline declared, when she emerged, that Eric would be a valuable partner for her in her present role. With a huge continent of diverse languages and needs, speedy and efficient computer connections were crucial to the operation of daily business in the European Parliament.

James confided that Caroline's job was high profile these days with the flood of emigrants from Africa and the Middle East arriving daily and the social network for supporting them stretching the capabilities of all the member nations. Caroline headed up a veritable tangle of charity organizations funded in a variety of ways to help alleviate the refugee situation. It was clear to his mother that James was exceedingly proud of his wife's capabilities. Their visit had to be short but it was all the sweeter for their delighted parents.

The California weather had been hot and humid when it wasn't fogged with pollution and a breath of cold, clear Scottish air was what Bev and Alan now longed for most.

Bev had another reason to hasten the journey to Oban. It seemed an age since she had spent any time with Anna. Jeanette had been reassuring about Ashley's care of the invalid. Cameron had supplied Jeanette an account of how she was coping, but Bev knew she would not be content until she saw Anna for herself.

Ashley waved goodbye to Edmund. He had insisted she use his first name although she felt uncomfortable about it. She watched as he expertly spun the car around and headed off to the other end of town. She took a deep breath then ran up the High Street searching for a ladies' clothing shop that might be supplied with the kind of sweater Anna needed. Fortunately, there was one place with a window display indicating preparations for the coming winter weather and she rushed inside hoping the proprietor was not busy. The owner came forward immediately and politely inquired if she could help.

Ashley had no time to browse the racks of garments so she quickly outlined her dilemma and found a sympathetic ear in the carefully dressed, older woman.

"Ach, I've been hearing what the poor woman has been going through. It's a crying shame, so it is.

My auntie is one of the A Plus Fairisle knitters and she has been right worried about Mrs. Drake. Please tell her she is not forgotten here in Oban. There's many who owe her a debt of gratitude for all she has done over the years."

"The sweater?" interrupted Ashley as delicately as she could. It looked like this soliloquy might go on for an hour and she needed to get groceries next.

"Of course." Sharon, of *Sharon's Boutique*, switched into sales style and soon uncovered the perfect cardigan, as she termed it, for an ailing woman's comfort. It was a deep mauve colour and had no buttons but wrapped around the body with a small hook fastening on the side. The length was enough to reach Anna's knees and the soft feel of the fabric confirmed it must be cashmere.

Sharon now completed the purchase with dispatch and Ashley was soon on her way through the town with only a quick glance at the seafront and harbour. She diverted along a side street and entered the large parking lot leading to the Tesco store.

Once she had a shopping cart in her hands, she buzzed around the store throwing in anything she thought might be needed for the next couple of weeks. She aimed to restock the cupboards and also find anything in the way of comforts for Anna. The oatmeal-based bath product Edmund had recommended was found in the Pharmacy and she added a lavender talcum powder and toilet water set along with a soothing shampoo and conditioner. Anna's hair had suffered from the long period without a proper wash. The pharmacist also suggested an alternative lotion to the messy calamine, for which Ashley uttered a sigh of relief. The washing would be simplified once she could dispense with the vivid pink product.

The cart was piled high when she reached the checkouts and she was hoping Cameron was nearby with a lift back to the farmhouse. As the goods were being loaded into bags she gave him a quick call and discovered he was only minutes away and would be heading for the store as soon as possible.

All in all, a very satisfying afternoon's work and there's fresh bread, meat pies and fish for a supper choice if Anna feels up to eating. I could whip up a fish casserole with cheesy mashed potatoes on top in no time.

She spotted Cameron's distinctive dark red Range Rover waiting right outside for her load, and they were soon on their way.

"I have news, Miss Ashley!"

"Oh, what's been happening?"

"I just delivered Mr. and Mrs. Matthews to your farmhouse with an ungodly amount of luggage."

"What? They're home already? Anna will be pleased to see them."

"Aye, you might say so. The puir wee soul was in tears when she opened the door. The ladies fell intae each other's arms right away. It was like a scene frae a movie."

She noticed how much Cameron sounded like his father, Grant, when overcome with emotion.

"Oh, Cameron! That's good news. You must have taken the Matthews' luggage back to their farmhouse or there wouldn't have been space for all this stuff I bought."

"That's right enough. Mrs. Drake told me to head back into town to collect you as soon as I dropped off the Matthews' bags and parcels. Alan gave me the keys so I could pop the bags indoors and turn on the heating for them."

"Excellent timing all round, I'd say."

"Aye, you could say so. I was glad to help. My father will be pleased to hear the news."

She settled back in the front seat of the Rover and felt a great relief. The whole awful period of Anna's illness was finally coming to a close with Bev's arrival. It had been a strain to be the one solely responsible for Anna's care but it had introduced her to Edmund Jansen. She let her mind drift to the vision of escorting him on the future visit to the romantic Glenmorie Castle. It should be interesting.

Ashley shooed Bev and Anna away to talk together while she made the fish casserole. Alan turned out to be a good help in the kitchen. He peeled potatoes, washed the vegetables and set the table all the while asking for updates on the town's gossip. Between them they got the grocery supplies stashed away and a custard made for, what in Britain they called 'afters'. Ashley could hear the rise and fall of voices from the lounge next door and when she caught the sound of Anna's laughter she knew the tide had turned and all would be well.

Rain was lashing on the windows but indoors it was cozy and warm with the Aga going full blast and the oven heat adding to the comfort level.

When the women were called to the table by Alan, wrapped in a chef's apron, Ashley saw that Anna was wearing her new sweater and looking much improved with the pretty mauve shade next to her face. And yet, having been away from her aunt for several hours, she also noticed that Anna had lost weight since her illness and beneath her high colour from the excitement of talking to her visitor, she was pale.

As soon as the meal had been eaten, Anna begged to go upstairs for a bath with her new products.

"I have had such a good time with my dear neighbours and friends, but Ashley will tell you this is the longest I have been out of bed since I got ill. Hopefully, I'll see you tomorrow, Bev, once you've unpacked and settled in."

The couple also expressed fatigue so Ashley told them to go before the dark descended, supplying them with a large golf umbrella that went back and forth between the farmhouses as required. There was not much kitchen clean-up to be done, thanks to Alan's help, so Ashley took the chance to have a quiet word with Bev before they left for the short walk home.

"What did you think about Anna?"

"Her spirits were high today but it's obvious this awful chickenpox has taken a lot out of her.

Quite frankly, I was shocked when I saw her at the door. I managed to hide my reaction when I hugged her to me, but she is thinner and looks much more frail than I have ever seen her."

Bev caught the troubled look on Ashley's face and quickly added, "Now don't be alarmed! We'll soon sort her out between us and there are others to help take the strain."

Ashley swallowed and tried to hide a tear that was pure relief on hearing the word 'we' coming from Bev's mouth.

The toll the last weeks had taken on her energy level was only now being felt. She had kept as positive as she could all the time Anna was so sick but now, at last, she could let go and admit what a trial it had been. When she had spoken by phone with her mother, Donna had expressed amazement at the way she had coped.

"Your Great-Aunt Anna is lucky you were available to help, Ash. Your publisher has contacted me several times asking where you were. I said you were in Scotland and that seemed to satisfy him. You had better give him a call soon.

Don't worry about your grandparents. I've been keeping them up-to-date with events. They send their best wishes to Anna, of course. Simon says to tell her his hip is giving him jip so he knows how she feels. And look after yourself, my girl. You don't want to come down with some dread disease from being overtired."

Ashley thought of these words as she turned out the lights and climbed upstairs to bed. She could hear Anna humming happily in the adjoining bathroom but, although she intended to stay awake until the bedroom door closed safely behind her aunt, she was fast asleep in minutes.

Chapter Ten

The phone ripped Ashley out of a deep sleep but before she could orient herself she heard Anna's voice responding. She flopped back onto her pillow and pulled the covers up over her ears. If Anna was able to take care of this call, she was content to let her do it just this once.

The next time she surfaced it was to find Anna by her bedside, dressed in her new sweater and a pair of cotton sweat pants and carrying a tray with a large mug of coffee that smelled divine.

"Now, just you sit there and drink this. I've been up for a while and I am feeling much better this morning. The bath last night was so refreshing and my hair looks almost decent again, don't you think?"

Ashley readily agreed and admired the silver strands curving around her face. She sipped the coffee twice, before asking who had called earlier.

"Oh, that was Gordon with great news. The baby has arrived. It's another boy and both he and Fiona are well. Gordon says he'll be either Neil or Craig. They'll decide when they've seen him at home and had a family conference. And Fiona says I've to get well soon so she can invite us to meet him. Fergus and Shona are delighted with their new brother and can't wait to get him home."

"That is good news, Anna. Now you have something special to work towards. Let's start with a good breakfast. I bought whole wheat granary bread from the bakery yesterday. I know it's your favourite and we'll slather it with butter and anything else you like. Do you think you can swallow that?"

"I think I could eat several slices, Ashley, thanks to all your efforts. I can never thank you enough, my dear girl, for all you have done. You have coped with all the work around this old place and I know what that means. I could never have managed to survive without you.

Now, don't start bubbling, as my mother used to say, or you'll set me off.

I'll let you get ready, Ashley, and please help yourself to the lavender set. The smell is amazing!"

It was a grand start to the day. The weather was cooperating and a pale sun was to be seen fighting its way through the clouds. Anna took it as a good omen. Her battle was almost over and today was the first of her recovery. She had abandoned the walking stick in preference for short walks around the house and up and down the stairs for exercise to strengthen her muscles. It was hard to remember how she had recently plodded up Wonderland Road after walking in the park in London. Hopefully, her muscles would now respond without too much delay. She was anxious to get back to life.

She had just returned to the kitchen from one of these forays when she spotted a van driving along the side of the house and parking in front of the garage.

"Ashley! It's Jeanette! I'll put the kettle on for tea."

Jeanette arrived in her usual style talking ten to the dozen and exclaiming how good it was to see them both.

"You must have felt you were in jail with a quarantine period like this. I have felt so frustrated at not being able to help but all that is over now. We have finally moved and everything is in place, I'm glad to say. I have no pressing jobs to do until well into next month so I am at your beck and call for whatever you need. My mother doesn't arrive here until nearer Christmas. Oh, the first thing is to give this place a thorough cleaning. It's overdue and I'll send the crew here next week. You two will come out for the day with me so they can scour out all the bad germs and give the place a proper going over. Perhaps we can go to the castle and visit the new babe? I hear it's a wee boy. Gordon will be so pleased.

Now, I see a pot of tea at the ready so let's sit down and you can tell me all your plans."

By the time Jeanette took her leave, both Anna and Ashley were ready for a nap. They had lived in comparative silence for so long, it was exhausting to cope with the speed of her speech and the plethora of ideas that spilled from her mouth.

"She's a force to be reckoned with, don't you think, Ashley? We added Jeanette to our original Canadian Samba group and she's been a great asset, especially for me. However, I think a short rest is in order now. I need to gather my strength if we are to be visiting the new baby soon."

Ashley agreed and planned to use the quiet time to do some preliminary planning for her book. After this she would call her publisher with the news that she had already started on the project. A slight exaggeration, of course, but she was reluctant to tell him the true story. Whatever happened, she and Anna must discuss the book's contents soon.

The discussion occurred sooner than Ashley had expected.

She had made the call to Canada and was back at her notes when Anna arrived in the kitchen and guessed what she was doing.

"You have been patient so long, Ashley. What do you suggest for your book's contents? Do you want me to write something for you, or would you prefer to ask questions for me to answer?"

"I think the latter would be easier for you. I can make quick notes at first but I will have to buy a recorder of some kind so as not to make errors with your accounts."

She turned to a fresh page of her notebook. "Shall we give it a try now and see how we manage? Tell me about your first meeting with Lawren."

Anna smiled and moved over to the padded bench by the window so she could look out at the rain-washed garden and think back to the beginning of it all.

"I suppose you can say it was art that brought us together. I had decided I wanted a painting or portrait of Helen Dunlop to hang in her house here as a tribute to her. The problem was how to do this as I had very few images of Helen to use as a guide. I advertised for an artist who might be interested in a challenging assignment and Lawren arrived at my door in London, on his bicycle, of course.

At first, I had no idea who or what he was and it was due to his perseverance that we connected at all. I'm afraid I was quite dismissive of him, suspecting him of being a young salesman of some kind. It was only after I had mentioned his name to Susan that I really found out how talented he was as a portrait painter. When I finally accepted his invitation and climbed up to his attic studio in the old house, I soon learned how intuitive he was."

"Lawren Drake's intuition is an acknowledged aspect of his talent. How did it show itself to you? It isn't an easy thing to describe."

"You are quite right. I didn't give it that label at first. I just caught the sense of something unusual in his glance. He seemed to look past my external appearance and delve into the depth of my feelings and intentions. It was not a comfortable experience, Ashley. I admit I was afraid of his ability to gauge my inner thoughts."

"I can imagine that would be a trifle upsetting for someone like you. Was it part of the 'golden gaze,' as I once heard you describe it?"

Anna's laughter rang around the kitchen. It was to Ashley, a sure sign of her recovery. That happy sound had been missing for some weeks now.

"Oh, I believe I did use that phrase and it's true. You knew him, Ashley. You fell under that gaze more than once. The very first time you met Lawren, he mentioned your future aspirations."

"I remember. We climbed Helen's Hill together and he simply listened to my young-girl-talk for a while. He did have an unusual eye colour but I think his listening skills were equally important."

"I agree. He never indulged in meaningless chatter. He listened intently. When someone does that, as effectively as he did, it makes the speaker more inclined to reveal things. Perhaps this is one secret of his intuition but there was more to it."

"What do you mean?" Ashley's pen was poised. She was ready for a new revelation and she was well aware the success of her book depended on these new revelations.

"I don't suppose you were ever told about the embarrassing encounter in a London coffee shop."

"Go on."

"Well, Lawren and I were meeting there so I could show him some of the few family photos I had.

That wasn't the embarrassing part. We were being spied upon by Susan and Alina which I did not like at all. I think it was the first time he held my hands in his, across the cafe table. I definitely felt something and it was not about the strength of his painter's grasp. It was a peculiar sensation of what I can only describe as 'rightness'. A feeling of coming home, I suppose. It sounds strange, I know, but it was an aspect of Lawren's mystery that he could make me feel that way when I was so uncertain about the portrait project, never mind the contact with a much younger man."

Anna's hand went to her throat. It was a gesture Ashley had observed before whenever her aunt was feeling emotional.

"Was there something else of significance about that moment?"

The older woman paused to think and her fingers automatically turned the thin small ring she wore on her right hand.

Ashley knew this ring had belonged to Anna's mother. It was one of the pair of rings she always wore.

Anna Mason Drake could definitely afford to replace, either or both of these rings, with something more expensive but she had never done so.

"He asked to hold this ring with its tiny flower shape composed of small diamond chips. I said nothing when I handed it over but he cradled it in his hands as if it were the precious Kohinoor diamond. He knew instantly it held great meaning for me. I now believe it was at that very moment he devised the notion to paint a triple project including my mother and Helen Dunlop. I can't prove it, of course, but it is entirely possible. I might have been able to verify his thoughts right then if we had not been interrupted by the two spies. Lawren was polite but he left quickly and I thought I would never see him again."

"Did that thought disturb you?"

"Not at first. My focus was on my own annoyance at the way we had been disturbed. Lawren had taken my photos with him and he had promised to return them, so eventually I understood there was to be another meeting and I began to look forward to it although with some apprehension. I did not know why I was so confused."

"Did your own intuition kick in then?"

"I suppose so. Or it could have been the beginning of the

attraction I felt that kept me moving forward with the unlikely project."

"So your next meeting was the one you mentioned just now, when you really understood about his intuition?"

"Yes. He had taken the photos and made a preliminary sketch of the three heads. The background was hazy but the faces stood out and I admit to being shocked when I saw them. It was uncanny how he had devised such detail from the meagre information in a few blurry old black and white images. Yet, something felt so right about what he had created. It hit me in the heart, if you know what I mean?"

"I think I do. It's something you just know is true although you can't really explain why."

"That's it exactly! I knew there was a talent here beneath the surface and the man wielding the pencils and brushes, was tapping into a force beyond the obvious."

Ashley took a moment to write down the exact quote. She was looking for phrases that might be a title or even a chapter heading for the book. She needed to go off now and transcribe what she had heard.

She wanted to capture the essence of Anna's memories. Her journalist's instincts told her this was priceless. So many people would be eager to learn what Anna knew about Lawren Drake.

"I think that's enough for now Aunt Anna. I will get this down on paper in a better form. Once I source a recording device we can go on for longer, if you are up to it."

"Of course, Ashley. It feels good to be talking about him this way. I can sense him much more clearly than I usually do." She paused to smile, then continued.

"Oh, I was thinking about something. Would you like to use the office in the lounge for a quiet spot to write in? It's rarely used nowadays. I have the key in a kitchen drawer here. It's yours if you want and you can lock it for complete privacy. And feel free to use the laptop computer in there. Like most people these days, I use my phone for everything. "

"That sounds like a wonderful idea. I can retreat there without disturbing anyone else who might be in the house. I remember it's a lovely space with the large window looking onto the rear garden and Helen's Hill. It's the perfect place for a writer."

Ashley took charge of the key and went at once to examine her new office. It was just as she had remembered. She plugged in the laptop and left it charging up. After her first real session with Anna, she was excited at the prospect of hours more to come.

Thank God the memories were still fresh and relevant.

It was not only the content that delighted her. It was such a privilege to spend this private time with her aunt. She was conscious, however, that obtaining the private times would become more difficult now that Anna's friends were keen to re-establish their connections.

Chapter Eleven

Ashley's prediction was correct. Bev's call the next day set the merry-go-round in motion.

Anna reported to Ashley that Bev had learned Fiona was back at home with the new baby.

"There's no more lingering in the hospital for days like Bev did when James and Eric were born in Canada. It's up and out now which suits Fiona fine. She wants us to come over as soon as we can.

Bev says she needs another day or so to set up her own household again but she is going into Oban to shop this afternoon and will take you with her if you want. I'll wait for Jeanette to call with a date for the house-cleaning crew. She'll take both of us to Glenmorie for the day and we can inspect the new house and the new baby boy. I can hardly wait to see all of them. Such a lovely family!"

Ashley could hear a happy note of anticipation in her aunt's voice at these plans. She would accept Bev's ride to town and look around for a recorder as well as cards and a gift for the new baby.

Anna was happy to stay put for another day. She had a plan to check through her wardrobe for suitable clothes for visiting Glenmorie and she would put a meat pie in the oven for their supper when Ashley returned. The rain and wind had blown away, bringing more settled weather, but the temperature was much colder and she did not want to catch a chill in her weakened state.

Anna also wanted to phone Alina and bring her up to date with the long period of her inability to communicate. There might be recriminations and she preferred to hear these on her own.

To Anna's relief Alina was not reproachful about the long absence. She was more concerned about the illness and Anna's recovery.

"Truly, I am well on the mend now. I promise not to rush things although I will admit to being tired of being shut up here when my objective was to enjoy time with friends again. I guess Rabbie Burns' claim 'the best laid plans o 'mice and men gang aft agley,' fits the case."

"As long as you are over the worst now, I won't complain too much but I am concerned about what might have happened if Ashley had not been with you and I feel guilty because I can't be there."

"Oh, Alina, please don't fret about that. I am glad you did not have to endure my misery but it has made me think more about our conversation regarding where we would choose to roost in our latter days."

"Surely, it wasn't that bad?"

"No, no! Giving my voice a rest for a week or two was not such a punishment. I was never in danger of dying and yet, I wonder what would have happened if I had need of hospital services. The medical care I got was excellent but a decent hospital is not close by as it would be in London, Ontario."

"Well, we can talk about that another time, Anna. You just concentrate on getting fit so you can see everyone. I am expecting full details on all that's been happening since my last visit."

Anna noted Alina's concerns and decided not to tell her about Ashley's book project and its effect on her. That might be a conversation for another day when she knew how it was shaping up. So far it had been pleasant to think about Lawren at the beginning of their romance but there was more to be told and some of it was still harrowing for her.

༺☙༻

Ashley was in the office transcribing her notes when the phone rang. She picked it up and was surprised to hear Edmund Jansen's voice.

"Ashley? I'm calling to let you know I have an entire afternoon off this week. I know it's short notice but I thought I would tell you, just in case you are free."

It was a jolt to force her mind from Anna's account of Lawren's intuition to figuring out why the doctor should be calling her. Then she remembered the prospective date at the castle.

"Oh, I can't say for sure, Dr. Jansen, but let me check for you and I'll call you back if it can be arranged."

She heard her words, and immediately thought they could not have sounded more formal. She had even reverted to his title rather than his first name. Before she could apologize, he murmured something noncommittal and the phone clicked off.

"Darn! Now I will have to contact Gordon."

She knew the number and was relieved to get a reply on the line after a couple of rings.

"Glenmorie Castle office; Donald here. How can I help?"

She realized at once that Gordon would be in the new house settling in Fiona and the baby and this was not the time to be asking for favours.

"Oh, Donald, it's Ashley, Anna Drake's niece. I'm sorry to bother you."

"Not at all, Ashley. I hear you have been a lifesaver lately for your aunt. I hope she is doing well now?"

"Yes, she is coming along, I'm glad to say. I was calling about another matter but I think it best to wait until a better time."

"As you wish, of course." There was a slight pause before he continued. "I do know I'll be asked questions about this call by the boss, so perhaps you should give me a clue?"

She was trapped now. There was nothing else to be done.

"Well, Donald, I was going to ask if I could bring a visitor to see the castle sometime. It's the new doctor, Edmund Jansen, but I know Gordon and Fiona have more than enough to deal with at the moment and doubtless there will soon be many visitors including my aunt and Jeanette McLennan."

"Och now, you are asking the right person about this, Ashley. I am in charge of the castle bookings these days and I can tell you there's nothing planned for the whole of this week. You are welcome to come by any day and I'll give your guest the tour. It's no trouble, and my cousin Angus says the young doctor has done wonders for his wife's arthritis, not to mention how he has helped you and Mistress Drake lately. Shall we say Wednesday afternoon?"

She recognized once again the networking system in a small community. Everyone knew everything that was going on. She would not be surprised if there was already some gossip about her trip to town in the doctor's car. No doubt speculation was rife. Donald seemed overanxious to set up this date for her.

"If you're sure it's no trouble, Donald."

"Absolutely, sure. Just come by the office and I'll have the keys ready."

The next task was to tell Edmund and try to reverse the poor impression she had left with him on their last call. Instead of the doctor, however, she reached the surgery receptionist and had to leave a message which was not what she wanted.

Another tasty bit of gossip to be circulated on the hot line.

Returning to her writing, Ashley half hoped Wednesday would not work out. This was getting complicated and she had more important things to do than swanning around in an old castle with a virtual stranger.

The writing had to be abandoned, finally, when Bev arrived with her car. Ashley ran upstairs to get her purse and tidy her hair. It would not do to be seen in Oban in an unkempt state now that her name was undoubtedly on the lips of local gossips.

She returned to the kitchen to find Bev and Anna in the midst of an update on how many changes had occurred in their mutual hometown.

"You wouldn't believe how London has grown, Bev. It seems as if every unoccupied corner is being used for another small development of townhouses. Alina and I are thankful Rosecliffe is walled on the east side and meets Springbank Road on the north, so no further building is possible. You wouldn't recognize most of the city, and as for the traffic! It's impossible to go anywhere during rush hours. We are glad we retirees can pick and choose our times to go out."

"I can imagine what you mean. After Los Angeles, Alan and I are so delighted we can return here to the peace of the countryside. You must feel the same way, Anna."

"I do, but it has been different while I was so ill. Anyway, we'll talk about that another day. Ashley has some important shopping to do. No doubt she'll tell you about it on the drive."

Ashley had not stopped to consider how she could capitalize on the private time with Bev. As one of the oldest of Anna's friends, it could be useful to outline the book idea and ask for Bev's opinion on Lawren and his impact on Anna's life. It was too good an opportunity to miss.

As soon as they were off the track and onto the main road she quickly filled in the details.

Bev's head remained forward with her eyes on the road but Ashley could tell she was surprised.

"I must say, I did not expect to ever hear Anna was willing to reveal aspects of her life with Lawren.

You must know how private a person she is, and always has been. I really feel I should say I hope you have not taken advantage of her weakened state, or even her gratitude for all you have done during her illness, to put pressure on Anna. We Sambas are very protective of her, you know."

Once more, Ashley was brought abruptly to a realization of how privileged she was to be allowed this insight into Anna's life. She knew she must proceed with caution if she was to get the kind of cooperation that would make her proposed book successful. She quickly decided to try to mend fences with Bev.

"I can assure you, Mrs. Matthews, that I am well aware of how fortunate I am to get this opportunity. I would never put pressure on my aunt and I will respect her boundaries totally. You must know how Lawren Drake's popularity as an artist has grown since his untimely death. There are many who long for more insight into his life; the kind of insight only Anna can reveal."

"Oh, I do understand the appeal, Ashley. Art fans appear regularly at my door and they have been known to climb on windowsills at Anna's place to try to get a glimpse inside."

She chuckled, and Ashley was relieved to hear the topic had a funny side.

"I shouldn't object, of course. Many's the farmhouse cream tea I have sold while avoiding answering impertinent questions from strangers. I suppose your book will eliminate some of the curious from arriving here. That's if you can get sufficient information from Anna to complete it. She could take offence if you get too close to private matters."

Ashley thanked Bev for her warnings and recognized she

was not going to get any intimate stories from this source. She turned her thoughts to the shopping trip and they rode the rest of the way in silence.

༄༅

Three hours later, they met up for a coffee in a restaurant with a fine view of the harbour. The tide was in and the strip of sand had almost disappeared. Bev had already stowed her purchases in her car and asked how Ashley had managed with her own list. They looked over the baby gifts Ashley had found and she was pleased to have Bev's approval of the small garments.

"I'm sure Fiona will love to have these smart new things for her son. It's a few years now since Fergus was a baby. What else did you find?"

"Well, I found a digital recording device but it will be a back-up to my smart phone that does record speech quite nicely. I am not going to push Aunt Anna to talk for long so I will transcribe her words as we go along. That will give me a sense of the shape of the book and of how we need to proceed."

"I hope I was not too discouraging before, Ashley. I don't disapprove of your book idea, it's just that I am very protective of one of my oldest friends. If Anna had not decided to keep the McCaig Estate Farmhouse, I would never have met Alan Matthews or have had the opportunity to live here in this beautiful country and bring up my boys here with the father figure they had lacked for many years.

I owe her a lot."

Ashley nodded her head and sipped her coffee. She decided to take a chance and offer Bev a preview of her writing to calm her worries. It was not something a writer usually did, as the structure of a book could change radically as it progresses, but she needed this woman on her side.

"If you wish, Bev, I could show you some of the preliminary pages so you could be assured of my deep respect for Anna Drake."

"No, that won't be necessary. I will be content to see the finished work like so many others around here, and elsewhere in the world."

Once again Ashley was reminded of her responsibilities. This book, if it ever came to be published, would have an audience far beyond Oban and with that realization came the understanding of her accountability to Anna's memories, her friends' concerns, and to the art world in general. It was a formidable prospect and one she had to tuck into the back of her mind. If she set out to meet the demands of such different readers she would be stymied at the start and the project would never be completed.

She took a deep breath, looked out at the view of Oban harbour and determined to do her best by focusing solely on her aunt and the privilege she had been offered in her exclusive access. She must go at her aunt's pace and not force her memories. It was a tricky thing to do but she was going to use every resource she had, both physical and mental, to make the entire process as easy as possible.

Anna Mason Drake deserved that at least.

Chapter Twelve

Wednesday arrived with only one short session with her aunt while they tried out the new recorder.

It was a small unit with a rechargeable battery and Ashley was pleased it did not take up space or look too imposing. She could switch it on and it worked silently without being too obvious.

They were seated in the kitchen when the conversation began. Ashley wanted to go on from their previous session so she had prepared a question for her aunt.

"As you got to know Lawren Drake, which was more important to you; your art idea or your personal connection?"

Anna laughed and drew a shawl around her as if to ward off the intrusive question. Ashley's heart quailed. Had she gone over the boundaries already?

"It's a good question Ashley. I don't know if I can give you a clear answer. You must understand that my feelings toward Lawren were quite mixed from the beginning. I can't deny there was a strange attraction that I couldn't explain, but I was not looking for a relationship. Certainly not one with a man I perceived to be much younger than myself. The very thought was ridiculous to me. And yet, I pursued the matter of the portrait even when I secretly felt it must be a disaster since I could furnish the artist with so little in the way of material he could work with."

"Was he not surprised to be invited to Scotland to continue with the portrait?"

"Now, that was the most impulsive thing I ever did. I hardly knew him and there I was paying for a plane ticket to fly him to a place he had never been in his life. He was surprised, all right, and he was not the only one. Alina was positively aghast at my decision. She suspected Lawren of all kinds of nefarious designs on me and my property. She held those suspicions for a long time. In fact, the turning point was when the portrait was finally revealed upstairs in the master bedroom to an audience of friends and family. Somehow, they could all see that each brushstroke was imbued with genuine love and concern for me. But, I suppose I am jumping ahead in the story."

"Oh, that's quite all right. It must have been a very special moment for you. No wonder you remember it so clearly." Ashley saw that her aunt's hand was covering her throat and her eyes were clouding over with distant thoughts.

"Let's leave it there for now. I have a date this afternoon at Glenmorie. I don't expect to see Fiona or Gordon but I will leave the gifts for the new baby with Donald after the tour of the castle.

Can I get anything from town for you Aunt Anna?"

"No, no, dear. I'm happy here in the kitchen. I'll phone Jeanette and arrange our visit to Glenmorie's new house for Friday perhaps?"

"Yes, that suits me very well."

She had hardly finished speaking when a knock came at the door and Dr. Jansen was revealed on the doorstep, wearing a casual sweater under his suit jacket.

"I thought I should check on the patient before we go," he said, by way of an apology.

Darn it! Ashley does not look ready to go. I am too early. She'll think I am overanxious.

"Oh, of course. I'll just go and get my things. Aunt Anna is through in the kitchen."

She quickly snatched up the recorder and fled upstairs to tidy up. He was early. Did that mean he was anxious to see her or that he was more concerned with his medical work, even on what was supposed to be a day off? She knew better than to keep a man waiting. Her grandfather was still a demon for punctuality even in his retirement years and her mother insisted he was even worse when she was a child. The necessity of being on time was ingrained into Ashley and she did not like to be keeping a busy doctor waiting for her.

Her jacket and purse were lying on the bed and her outdoor shoes were on the carpet underneath. She grabbed a scarf in case of wind or rain and glanced in the mirror over the fireplace to see what she looked like to a stranger.

Her hair had grown longer since she arrived in Oban and it curled around her earlobes. She was losing the remains of her Canadian tan and she had also lost weight during her nursing stint. She turned her head from side to side to see if she had acquired cheekbones as a result, and was pleased to find that was the case. Her hazel eyes sparkled as usual and she concluded she didn't look too bad at all. Good enough to impress a local doctor, if, indeed, she needed to impress him.

Edmund Jansen was pleased to see Anna Drake looking so much better. She had made a good recovery from chickenpox and seemed to be coping with nothing more than a certain weakness of the major muscle groups. He agreed with her intention to stay indoors until the weather had improved and encouraged her to eat well in the meantime. During their conversation, he was listening for Ashley's steps on the stairs. He felt uncertain of his reception and was well aware of how uncomfortable it might be to spend time with someone who was possibly meeting an obligation to him because of his care of her aunt, and who really had no special interest in him. On the other hand, he was conscious of the fact he had not had the opportunity to meet many young women since his practice occupied so much of his time. It also occurred to him that this particular young woman was not a local resident. If this afternoon's visit turned out to be a disaster, Ashley Stanton would eventually return to Canada and he need never be reminded of his failure again. It was a reassuring thought.

"There you are, Ashley," exclaimed her aunt. "Do take your raincoat and an umbrella in case the weather turns wet. Have a good time at Glenmorie and tell them I'll be coming soon with Jeanette."

Ashley did as she was told and soon followed Edmund down the path to his waiting car. It was a much smaller vehicle than the others she had been in and she was, by necessity, in much closer contact with the driver. The initial moments were taken up with directions to the castle and Ashley took over the conversation as they bypassed Oban town and arrived on the main road north.

"Have you seen many Scottish castles, Edmund?"

"Not really. I've been to a few on the east coast like the ruins of Linlithgow and to Delgatie Castle, but not since I was a child. Much of my time was taken up with medical studies. My folks are not wealthy so I needed to work for financial help; scholarships and the like. Holidays were scarce and far between."

So he's always been a hard-working man. That speaks well for him.

"I went to university in Calgary myself and I know what it is to have to meet high standards. My mother, Donna, is a bit of an unsettled character. My grandparents, Anna's brother Simon and his wife Michelle, were my mainstay while my mother and father backpacked all over the world."

"That's interesting. We have had very different upbringings I suppose. What did you study?"

"Oh, English Lit. mostly, but I ended up in journalism when I saw no future in university teaching."

"So, you are a reporter or an author, or both?"

"Exactly! I can turn my hand to either when required."

"Which draws you to Oban at the moment?"

The questions were getting a bit too close for Ashley's comfort. The fewer people who knew about her writing project with her aunt, the better. They had just turned on to the approach road to Glenmorie so she diverted Edmund's query with further instructions.

"Oh, we're almost there. You will see the tower house rising above the fir trees in just a moment. We can park on the driveway and I am sure Donald will meet us with the keys. Fiona and Gordon recently moved to a new family house they built. I think the castle is unsuited for a young family, as you will see."

As expected, Donald was waiting for them.

"I saw the car when you entered the driveway by the main road. I was upstairs checking on the windows. It's a fine day so far. It'll be good to give the old place an airing. Come away in, doctor. This'll be your first visit?"

They shook hands and Donald took a good look at the young doctor's face. He was known as a person who could read a face well. Ashley wondered what he made of Edmund Jansen.

"Yes. It's a fine-looking place. I can see it's been kept in great shape which is unusual these days.

"Aye. There's not so much money around for maintenance of old buildings. Many a castle or mansion has been sold to foreigners. If the Laird and his lady did not have such a love of the place and a determination to preserve it, I fear it would have fallen into ruin by now."

Edmund exchanged a glance with Ashley. She seemed to agree with this conclusion. He had not met the Laird and his Fiona but he could tell from Donald's tone of voice, which matched Ashley's prior conversation, that the couple was more than just his employers.

This was proved to be true when they arrived at the top of

the steep set of stairs into the main hall of the castle. Donald was giving his well-rehearsed spiel about the historical, defensive reasons for such an elevated living area but Edmund hardly heard. His attention was taken by the impressive room stretching the width of the building with its ancestral paintings on the walls interspersed with a selection of fine targes and swords. There was a massive fireplace and the requisite tartan, high-backed chairs before it, but the polished table adorned with tall candle sconces demanded the most admiration.

"Do you host dinners at this table?" he asked, as soon as Donald had taken a breath.

"Indeed we do. Ashley will know of a lovely Canadian lady, Valerie Westwood, who escorts private tours in Scotland. She brings her group here for a special occasion and they enjoy a traditional meal in this hall. It's always a great success."

"I'm sure it is. This is a magnificent setting. Who keeps the silver looking so bright?"

It was an unusual question for a man to ask and Ashley was initially surprised and even more so at his explanation.

"I ask, because I had a job in a museum in Aberdeen when I was a student. One of my jobs was to clean the silver, both the flat wear and the decorative display pieces. I have intimate knowledge of how messy and precise that work has to be."

"You are right there, sir. Our housekeeper does not do so much these days as her knees are giving her trouble, but she had the help of a lassie from Oban, who she is teaching. Perhaps you would give her a tip or two?"

"Oh, no! My time is taken up with a different kind of activity. I'll leave that task to others, if you don't mind."

All three laughed at this and the tour continued in a lighter vein now Donald had the measure of his listener. Ashley was able to add in a few pointers about sword play as they climbed the spiral stone stairs to the bedrooms above the hall. She had not previously been on this private floor and she looked around with interest. The master bedroom had a huge bed with carved wooden headboard and footboard. She suspected it might once have borne a superstructure supporting a canopy, but that was gone now. The room had been denuded of personal touches which had likely been moved to the new house. With its whitewashed walls and slate floor it had the appearance of a forlorn place despite the alcove windows and the large chest at the foot of the bed. She supposed it was not necessary to decorate a room that was used mainly in the dark. It seemed to fit the Scottish bent toward the practical rather than the overtly showy.

The other three bedrooms were now even more stark and the small bathroom had clearly been added on by stealing a section of the stairwell. Ashley did not blame Fiona for wanting a much more friendly place for her young children to sleep.

"Would you be wanting to climb up to the ramparts to see the fine view over the land?"

Donald's question prompted Ashley to fasten up her jacket and retrieve the ever-useful headscarf she had tucked into a pocket. The crenelated roof was indeed high above the surrounding land and the wind whipped Edmund's dark hair around his head. He didn't seem to mind, but she had a fear of great heights and stood back against the door leaving Edmund to venture around the perimeter with Donald as he pointed out the various areas of the estate where fishing and hunting were allowed and the stands of mixed tree varieties were planted that were returning the land to the forests of ages past.

"So, Donald, can we get a glimpse of the new house you mentioned? I think it must be something special to compete with this tower castle."

"Well the Laird's idea was to blend the house into its surroundings in such a way that you would not see it from the castle. If you follow the line of the river over to your left, you will just be able to see a part of the roof."

Edmund looked where his guide had indicated but he was unable to detect anything roof-like in the sea of green in the distance.

Donald waited a moment or two then put him wise to the joke he was playing.

"*Dinna fache*, laddie! You're not supposed to be able to see it at all! That's the whole point. Part o' the roof is green turf where wildflowers will be growing on it in the spring. The other part has these big photo voltaic panels that store the sunshine. Those point to the south of course. You'd be needing binoculars to see any of it at all, at all!"

He went off, chuckling, to lead the way back to ground level. Neither of them noticed that Ashley had not moved from the doorway. Edmund gripped her shoulder as they descended in single file. He murmured his thanks in her ear. She smiled and nodded, smelling the fresh air that still surrounded him, but she did not turn around. The descent was treacherous as it was designed to be very narrow and the stone steps were only wide enough for feet at one particular point near the outer wall.

When she was back on solid ground again, Ashley saw a huge dark brown dog waiting with its tongue lolling out. Donald did not seem to be worried by the sudden appearance and she remembered talk about a giant guard dog at the castle.

"Is this the famous Hector?" she asked.

"Ah, no, Hector himself is gone these many years. This would be Hamish, who is a descendant. He is not exclusively his master's dog as Hector was, but he is a good guard for Fiona and the children. I'm thinking they must be nearby."

Donald turned to survey the cobbled yard adjacent to the castle and waved toward a cluster of children near the estate office.

"I see the young master and his school pals. I'll be off now.

It's been a pleasure to meet you, doctor, and to see you again Miss Ashley. I hear there's to be a house tour soon. Mistress Fiona is looking forward to that."

"I may not be here for that event, Donald, but I am sure it will go well. How is the new baby doing?"

The older man's weathered face split into a massive grin as he replied. "The wee bairn is a strong laddie for certain sure. You might hear his cries in Oban when he gets going. A fine pair of lungs he has."

They took their leave and Edmund watched as Hamish followed Donald across the yard.

"That's the biggest dog I have ever seen. I am glad he's well trained. I was shaking in my shoes when he sniffed at me. He could have bowled me over in a minute if he had stood on his hind legs."

"Not a dog lover, then?" observed Ashley. She felt a trifle pleased that he had a weakness. It made him seem more human somehow.

"Well, let's say I prefer dogs below my knees in size. Now, where can we have a cup of tea and a chat about you, Miss Ashley? I suspect you know much more about me than I know about you. I think it's time to address the imbalance."

They had their tea and scones in an Oban restaurant. Ashley noticed curious glances toward their table and several local people made a point of greeting the doctor. They nodded at her but were not about to ask who she was. She surmised she would be labelled as 'an in-comer', which was close enough to the truth. Perhaps, when she was seen out and about with her aunt, she would be accepted as part of Anna's group.

Edmund did not notice the curious, sidelong looks, he was too busy trying to extract information from his companion. She was not making this easy for him. In fact, he thought she was acting like someone who had a secret to keep. She was quite open about her family in Canada and about her love for

Scotland, but when it came to the topic of her work, she would swiftly change the subject.

A mystery woman! I am trained in solving medical mysteries. I can use my skills to decipher what she is trying to conceal. That's if she is willing to spend time with me again.

On the ride back to the McCaig Estate farmhouse there was a pleasant feeling of ease between them. Edmund cast around in his mind for an excuse to see Ashley again. He was limited by his busy schedule and by his lack of knowledge of the surrounding area, but he felt he had to come up with some kind of invitation before he deposited her at the red door. If he left it too long he could not capitalize on the comfort level they had obtained so far.

"Ashley, do you know of a place not too far away where I could walk in the hills? I need to get a bit of exercise after driving around to see patients or crouching over a desk for hours. I am no mountain climber, of course, but the countryside is very appealing on the west coast."

She wondered if he was being naïve or if he had not truly looked around when he came to the farmhouse. Helen's Hill was the obvious nearby climb and she was the obvious one to show it to him.

She let a moment pass while she considered if she wanted to see him again then, jumped in with both feet, surprising herself as much as she surprised the doctor.

"Well, the islands you can see out in the bay are the places I would recommend. Mull and Iona are the nearest but they may take more of your free time than you can afford. For a quick climb you could come up to the top of the steep hill behind Anna's house here. There's a well-worn path which makes it easy and once on the top you can explore for quite a distance. I haven't been up there for a while but the views are magnificent all the way out to the sea."

It was exactly the opening he had wanted. He came around the car and opened the passenger door for her.

"Thank you for today. I really enjoyed your company. If

you will agree to join me on the path you mentioned, I would be delighted to explore this area. May I call you when I have some time off?"

She could hardly refuse now she had been so effusive about the benefits of the climb.

"That would be good, Edmund. It's been an interesting afternoon. Keep an eye on the weather. Being caught on the top of a hill in the rain is not something I would recommend."

"I'll do that. Thanks again. We'll talk soon."

Off he went after turning the car expertly on the track and barreling down toward the main road. She stood at the gate watching, and wondering if she had oversold her prowess in climbing. There were no hills to speak of on Prince Edward Island and Edmund Jansen, a Scot, was undoubtedly more accustomed to hill walking than she would ever be. There was always the chance the weather would descend and prohibit the ambitious scheme. As she turned toward the front door she could not decide if she would be relieved at that scenario or if she would be disappointed.

Chapter Thirteen

❧

Jeanette McLennan was as good as her word. She deftly co-ordinated her cleaning crew's availability, Fiona Campbell's baby-feeding schedule, and Anna's recovery rate, and called the farmhouse to announce the date of the visit to Fiona's new house.

Anna was thrilled. She felt as if she was given parole from prison. A very comfortable prison, of course, but one nonetheless. She could hardly wait to see Fiona again. It had been too long since her last visit to Scotland and she was eager to see the children and especially the new little one. Lacking a child of her own, Anna always considered Fiona as her daughter of the heart and so her children were like grandchildren to her.

"I am so grateful you shopped for presents for the children, Ashley. I don't want to arrive empty-handed, as they say here. The older ones will be happy to play with their new gifts and we can have peace to visit with Fiona and the baby."

"Ah, about that, Aunt Anna, I think I will stay here, if you don't mind. I won't get in the way of the cleaners. I'll be in the office working on our latest recording. You and Fiona have lots of catching up to do and Jeanette will bring you back here afterward. I really need the time to work."

"Of course you must do that, Ashley. There will be other occasions to meet Fiona. Can I leave you to load the dishwasher? I want to look out clothes for the excursion. I am so excited about finally getting out in the world again."

Ashley collected dishes from the kitchen table and smiled at the sight of her aunt skipping up the stairs like a young thing. It was a tribute to her determination to recover her strength and to the walks around the garden and the rest of her property she had been doing daily for the last week. Ashley estimated she could relinquish her role as nurse at last and return to her professional mode. It would be good to get a long spell of time alone, to pull together the preliminary document, especially after last night's session. She itched to hear the recording again and complete her notes.

After admiring her aunt's outfit for the day, and ensuring she had a warm coat and hat to wear, she bade farewell to Jeanette, assured the cleaners she would be no trouble, and shut the office door with a satisfactory click. She was alone at last. She started the latest recording and picked up her notebook with the excitement that comes from anticipation. If the story her aunt had told last night was as dramatic as she remembered, it would make her book a 'must read'.

"We had debated for a long time if we should marry. I knew Lawren was sensitive to my feelings about the difference in our ages and he was reluctant to do anything that might be construed as benefitting from this divorced woman's property. I was equally conflicted. In many ways it seemed easier to keep things as they were. We were happy in each other's company and we grew closer every day.

It wasn't until we had actually slept together that I felt it necessary to legitimize our relationship in the eyes of our friends and associates. Not that they had any idea we were at that stage. I was not about to shout it from the rooftops despite how I felt about having a man in my life after so many years alone."

"If it isn't too intrusive, Aunt Anna, how did you feel?"

"I never expected to feel again the emotions Lawren Drake awoke in me. It was as if I was reborn in some ways. I felt lighter, younger, happier, more positive, jubilant, and a whole lot more that I can't even express. Who would have thought a woman of my advanced years could act and feel like a teenager in love? I knew the euphoria could not last forever but, unlike a teenager, I also knew I could survive and relish the stages of more settled emotions that would result from our initial passion.

Alina was watching both of us like a hawk. She would have pounced on Lawren if she even suspected he was taking advantage of me but she saw how happy he made me and she had, at last, to admit defeat."

"Were there others who were initially fearful of your closeness to Lawren Drake?"

"It's hard for me to say. I met his father eventually and he was pleased his son had something and someone in his life other than his obsession with his art, but I was not a part of his professional associations. I doubt any of his fellow artists knew about me until the paintings and drawings were seen in art galleries. We were, in our different ways, quite private people. Our love was known to only a few."

"But didn't you two have big parties to celebrate your union? I remember my grandfather talking about the one in your London home and wasn't there another here in Scotland?"

"You are quite right, Ashley. We decided to gather our friends together separately, on each side of the Atlantic, but our actual wedding ceremony was a very private affair at which none of them were present."

"What? I didn't know this. I just presumed your Samba friends were there."

"No. We couldn't decide whether to do the deed in Scotland or in Canada. Whichever we chose, there would be people who were disappointed. So we went to a place that had great meaning for us and with the help of George McLennan, we obtained a license and married in secret."

"You mean, *no one knew*?"

"That's right. No one knows to this day. We refused to talk about it and some thought we just had a party and the actual marriage never took place. We let them think what they wanted. We had done what suited us best."

"Well, I am surprised all right, and yet, it speaks to the unique style of you two as a couple.

Dare I ask more about the secret ceremony?"

There was a pause on the recording and Ashley remembered how she had held her breath while her aunt considered her response.

"I suppose it doesn't matter now. It was our own special secret but I can share it now, since he has gone. It was a magical day in a magical place and I will never forget one moment of it. If others learn what we did together it can't possible tarnish that day.

We took the journey to the holy isle of Iona which we had taken when we were at the first tentative stages of our romance. It was there by the crystal sea of The Bay At the Back of the Ocean where we picnicked and Lawren drew my face while I dozed with eyes shut."

"Oh, that must be the sketch in the beautiful frame upstairs. I have often admired it. You looked so relaxed and youthful, like a young girl."

"It was how he always saw me. How can I explain what it is to be loved by a man who saw inside me my best, most optimistic self, long before it was tainted by pain and disappointment? It was like being reborn to be with him."

"That's a very powerful image."

Ashley immediately planned to get permission to use the sketch in her book and the thought recurred when she got to this part of the recording. She made a note in her notebook but returned to listen closely. The next part of their conversation was the most amazing of the entire session, perhaps of the entire book.

"We had a suitcase with us containing a change of clothes. We had booked a small Bed and Breakfast hotel in the town, facing the ferry terminal.

In the early morning of the following day while the mists were still wreathed around the buildings, we crept out and made our way to the Abbey. Lawren wore a dark suit he had borrowed from someone and I had on a long dress of a material he chose for me. Over the dress I had a warm wool shawl and I had flowers in my hair that we picked from the roadside on our way.

A monk awaited us, but the Abbey was silent and empty as we stood by the altar. The ceremony could not have been more sacred or more simple. It was a blessing and a promise in an ancient place so holy that I felt the weight of the years and the prayers that emanated from the very walls.

We made our vows to each other and it was done.

A couple who worked in the Abbey gift shop were summoned to provide witnesses. Lawren took the signed document, folded it and placed it in an inside pocket of his suit jacket. The evidence meant nothing to us. The experience was everything.

When we emerged, arm in arm, the sun had risen and the mist had dissolved. Around us were the symbols of Saint Columba's faith; Celtic stone crosses, the graves of kings and above all the seabirds calling and crying his praises to heaven.

It was a moment of wonder, dedication and love and I have never felt anything to compare with those feelings, before or since."

Another silence occupied several minutes of the recording. Ashley picked up her pen to note her own feelings during this period but again her eyes were moist and she could scarcely see the page before her. It was such an intimate moment. So much so that she knew she would not change one word of her aunt's account. It spoke for itself.

As a journalist she wondered if there was a wedding breakfast back at the B&B and where the dress went that Anna had worn and if they said anything to anyone at all when they returned to Oban or if George McLennan maintained his professional discretion forever.

She imagined their two faces told the tale that day to anyone who saw them, but she would not press her aunt to reveal more details.

Her account was perfect, as it stood.

So, what next? She decided to prepare a kind of map of the book in a chronological order so she would know if there were significant gaps she needed to fill. The finished work would not likely be strictly chronological, but it would be an interim aid to clarity.

She found a program on the laptop that allowed the kind of outline she wanted and spent several minutes mapping out a lifeline. She also started a list of notes for reference. It included significant moments in Lawren and Anna's relationship that would be important for the book. On this list she added Lawren's death scene and as she typed the words she knew it was something she was reluctant to even ask about. As far as she knew, Anna Drake had never discussed the time and place of her husband's death. Ashley knew only that it was sudden and traumatic and that Anna was present.

If she had enough of her aunt's confidence, it was possible this private information might be shared.

At the very thought of this coup, she drummed her fingers on the edge of the keyboard in excitement.

First the marriage revelation, and now the hoped-for detail of Lawren's death; it would make the proposed book a best seller.

Once again, Ashley had to calm her expectations. She must not push her aunt beyond what she was comfortable sharing. It could bring the entire project to a crashing halt and that was unthinkable.

Anna Mason Drake's account might not be her only

source. There were others who might be persuaded to contribute but in the end it would be Anna's choice what, of her own life story, was allowed to be in print for the world to read.

※

It was not her usual custom to be so talkative. Anna sat beside Jeanette in her Design company van and chattered away like a monkey. She felt released from her long confinement and noticed every single thing she saw on the way to Glenmorie Castle.

"Is that a new shop on the promenade? I see a For Sale sign on that lovely Victorian Hotel right by the shore. Are the couple who owned it retiring? Just look at the seagulls clustering around that fishing boat! Isn't it a lovely fresh day for our outing? I am so grateful to you, Jeanette, for arranging this.

I know how busy you are."

"Nonsense! I am delighted to spend time with you, Anna, and to see you looking so well again. You are not the only one who is anxious to see Fiona and the new wee one. Remember, also, that I have been moving house lately and that has kept me from seeing the new Campbell residence. We'll enjoy it for the first time together, and I can't wait. George says it's something special although, as usual, he is closed-mouthed about any detail. I guess one of his clients is in the building business and mentioned how forward-thinking the young Campbells have been.

Not far now. Is that a maple tree flaming red over in the forest? It reminds me of Canada, seeing that sight here in early November. There's nothing to compare with the colour of our homeland's trees in the fall."

"Do you miss Canada, Jeanette?"

"Truthfully, Anna, I rarely think about it. My life is here with George and the children and as soon as my mother arrives from Vancouver to live with us, I think my last real link with Canada will be severed.

There will always be memories, of course, and they are good ones. What more can I ask?"

Anna tucked away her friend's comments for later discussion with Alina.

They were now bumping along the side road that led to the castle drive and Jeanette was busy steering the van over potholes filled with the recent rain.

"Oh, I see the castle ramparts ahead! We'll be there soon."

The gates were open and as soon as they came to a halt on the circular driveway in front of the castle, Donald emerged and climbed into the van's back seat.

"Welcome, ladies! The Laird and Lady Fiona are waiting for you. I'll show you the way to the new house and then go back by a shortcut through the woods to watch for the children arriving from school."

There followed a series of turns and twists as they were directed on secondary roads and lanes to the depth of the forest. Jeanette was wondering if the next turn would mean ducking under the branches of tall fir trees when they suddenly emerged into a clearing on a rise filled with light.

There was no need for an announcement as the house lay before them in all its splendour. It was totally different from what Anna had expected. It was square in shape, clad in wood, with a flat roof covered in a green mat with panels of what she recognized as solar conductors tilted toward the sun. The house had two floors, large windows and an overhang that shaded the balconies on the upper level. To the side of the house, gardens stretched downhill toward the surrounding trees and there seemed to be a pond with tall reeds growing in and around it.

Before she could absorb any more, Fiona, with baby in her arms, was hauling open the van door and crying out, "Come out of there this minute, Anna. I can't wait another second to hug you."

It was a joyous reunion and a few tears escaped. The baby did not seem to mind being crushed between his mother and the stranger and only gave a hiccup in protest.

Fiona handed her son to Anna and led the way toward her new home.

"Come in, come in! We can't wait to show our green house to you both. We are very proud of it."

"But, how can you live so far in the forest? How do you get electricity and sewer services?"

Jeanette was asking the practical questions that were on the edge of Anna's mind, now occupied with the weight and warmth of the tiny baby, Neil, in her arms.

"We don't need those services which is why we can live in this beautiful spot."

Gordon stepped out of the front door and smiled a welcome. "I've been instructed to give visitors the functions tour. Step this way and I'll point out the features of our Net Zero house.

All four positioned themselves by the front entrance while Gordon Campbell explained how the roof panels provided electric power which heated water in a storage tank filled by rain water. Waste water from washing, baths and toilets was diverted to the pond where it was filtered by the reeds and eventually made its way back to the stream that ran into the river near the property.

"The house is built on a concrete pad which absorbs heat and regulates the overall temperature of the house. The walls are made of wood struts from our own trees and the insulation is recycled newspaper and sheep's wool. The windows are triple glazed, capture all the light and the overhangs shade the interior in the summer."

"That's the basics," interjected Fiona, with a voice that echoed her husband's pride. "But there's lots more to it inside. Come and see how comfortable it feels."

Fiona was right, thought Anna, as she stepped into a large open kitchen that felt as warm as any Aga-heated farmhouse.

It was painted in light, bright colours and had a floor of polished concrete with colourful scatter mats indicating the seating and playing areas. There was a whole wall of storage and book shelving and the views from all the windows were spectacular.

"So this is the Eco House you two always wanted?"

"Indeed it is," said Gordon, as he retrieved his son and waved the women upstairs.

Jeanette soon discovered the bookshelf wall was the outer part of the staircase that wound around and deposited them on an upper gallery off which there were four bedrooms with even more spectacular views to the rear of the property.

"But how are you going to keep the children's noise from disturbing you down below?" she asked.

"Well, when the doors are open we can hear what the older two are up to and when it's time for sleep, the doors are double-insulated."

"Very wise," was Jeanette's comment to Fiona. "You seem to have thought of everything and it could not be more different than the draughty old castle with all those stone stairs."

Fiona placed her arm around Anna's shoulders and said, "We loved our old castle but it was not the place to bring up three children; which reminds me to show you the family bathroom and our ensuite.

What luxury it is *and* it's designed to save water."

When they had finished admiring the bathroom's shining modern fixtures and the underfloor heating, Gordon called them to come for tea, then excused himself as he had estate business to attend to, leaving the women to ooh and aah over the new baby and demand all the details of his birth from Fiona.

"Och, he was no trouble at all. Slipped out like a wee fish and cried for only a moment. Gordon was there for the birth and he was duly thrilled to have another son."

"I think Neil is more like you, Fiona, than like a Campbell."

"He has my colouring, I think, although his eyes could change to Gordon's grey. He's a grand wee chap and he sleeps and eats well. Shona is fascinated with him and wants to help every minute when she's home, but Fergus says he'll be more interested when his brother can play with him."

Fiona suddenly turned serious and, with a glint in her eye, asked Jeanette if she would mind watching the baby, who was now sleeping peacefully in a Moses basket on the floor near where the trio sat.

"I have something to show Anna and I need to take her away for a few minutes."

"Off you go! I am perfectly content right here with this wee lamb."

Anna followed along as Fiona led her to the back of the house and a rear exit where Fiona described a play area and garden they were to build in the following spring. She did not stop there but moved onto a gravel path at the end of which Anna could see a shed or garden house sheltering under the tall firs that sheltered the property.

"Now, I don't know how you will feel about this, Anna. I don't want you to feel pressured in any way."

"What are you talking about, Fiona? You are sounding very mysterious."

"You'll see."

The door opened and Anna could see nothing in the dim interior until her eyes adjusted from the bright light outdoors. She gazed around and found only a few tools and some bins holding empty plant pots.

She was about to ask what she was supposed to be looking for when she heard the tiniest sound; a small squeak. At once her mind was flooded with memories of the time she had known just such a small squeaking sound very well.

"Fiona!" she gasped. "What have you done?"

"Nothing, really. You can blame Mother Nature. We found this little mite abandoned and close to death. It's a hybrid, so not subject to the species preservation laws. I checked with the vet, it's still Callum Moir by the way, and he confirmed our conclusion."

Anna moved forward. She was compelled to see for herself. There, in the bottom of a deep cardboard box lay a kitten with the brindled brown colouring, small ears and brushy tail that identified it as a Scottish Wild Cat hybrid. Its mother must have been a stray cat that contributed only the slightly smaller size, as the father's features were so strong.

There was silence in the shed other than the sound of their breathing, until Anna said with a quaver in her voice, " Fiona, is it really another Sylvester after all these years?"

"I'm afraid not. This one is a Sylvia, if you don't mind another female in your household? I know how you missed Morag."

Anna longed to say a fervent 'Yes', but practical problems arose, preventing her from doing what she wanted.

"But, I will be leaving in a month or two. What will happen then?"

"I have talked to Bev. She is happy to resume your old system of the cat going back and forth between houses. Bev says she will be glad to have a cat around again to keep down the mice that creep inside in the autumn."

"Oh, I can hardly believe this! Remember the old days when we nursed Sylvester in the kitchen cupboard and tried to keep him safe inside?"

"Of course, I do. That was a real adventure for us. It was the first time we conspired together to defeat bureaucracy, and the experience gave me a taste for rebelling that remains to this day. Just ask Gordon!

As for Sylvia, you need to know I am encouraging the children to come and play with her briefly, to accustom her to the sound of human voices and the smells also."

"Won't they want to keep the kitten for themselves?"

"Well, I have explained it wouldn't be safe for the new baby and we have enough already to care for. They are content with that. They have the whole forest world of animals to observe here and the river otters are particular favourites."

"The children would have visiting privileges, naturally," added Anna.

Fiona's eyes opened wide.

"Do you mean you agree to take Sylvia?"

"Of course I do! How could I refuse? Morag's window seat is waiting for her whenever you feel she is ready to be moved."

"I am so glad. I can't imagine a better home for her. Now that's decided, let's go back and you can tell me everything that has happened since I saw you last. Every single thing now; leave nothing out!

Chapter Fourteen

It was a different Anna who returned home in the van with Jeanette. She felt more settled and calm after their long, happy visit with Fiona's family. Jeanette had asked more practical questions about food supplies for the Campbells if they were intending to live as independently as possible, and received a lengthy list of resources like vegetable and fruit gardens soon to be planted and cared for by the older children to which their parents would add fish from the river and venison from the deer cull in the winter.

"We are a long way from the nearest grocery shop," explained Fiona, "but the children go back and forth to Oban for school so I can get supplies that way, if necessary."

In conclusion, both Anna and Jeanette admired the enterprise of the Campbells and loved the idea of them living in the forest on a huge estate that provided all their needs.

"I'll be taking my two to visit as soon as I can winkle George out of his office for an hour or two. We all need to see what self-sufficiency looks like in this new age that's coming."

Anna thought she was not likely to be alive in the new age to which Jeanette referred. For now she was glad to have the conveniences of her big stone estate house. She felt a sense of real homecoming as they approached up the lane. Jeanette came inside to inspect the cleaning work that had been done earlier, and she soon expressed satisfaction with the results. Ashley emerged from the office when she heard their voices and she gave every evidence of having been hard at work. She was stretching her shoulders and massaging her hands.

"Well, hello again, you two! You *have* been gone a long time. How was your first outing, Aunt Anna?"

"To tell the truth, Ashley, I am feeling a bit tired now after all the excitement of the day. "I'll go up and get changed and maybe we can have something light for supper. I need an early night, but I have something to discuss with you before I sleep."

Ashley thought she saw a conspiratorial glance pass between the friends but there were no further explanations. She went to the front door with Jeanette and discovered the air had cooled remarkably and the night had arrived while she was working in the office. She shivered as she waved farewell, then quickly closed the door and went into the cozy kitchen to find something for their supper.

She discovered a covered plate with muffins and a container of applesauce sitting on the table attached to a note asking for a review of the cleaning service.

"Smart move," she declared. She was tired from her day's writing efforts and cooking a meal at the end of the day was not appealing. She would add cheese, butter and grapes to the muffins and see if that satisfied Anna's appetite.

Tonight was obviously not going to be an opportune moment to advance the story of Anna's life with Lawren Drake but perhaps the topic her aunt wanted to discuss would lead to some other useful item for the book contents.

As soon as Anna had finished a muffin and a large mug of tea she introduced the subject of a new member of the family at the McCaig Estate farmhouse.

"Do you mean a kitten?" asked Ashley, with her surprise showing clearly. This was not what she had expected.

"Not just *any* kitten, Ashley. You must remember hearing about Sylvester, the Scottish Wildcat Fiona and I raised in this very kitchen years ago."

"Of course I remember the stories, but wouldn't a kitten mean a lot of work for you?" She was actually thinking of the time it would take from her writing project if her aunt was running after an active kitten.

"Fiona has promised to raise Sylvia until she is independent and at least partly house trained. The Campbell children will look after her for me until then. Callum Moir, the local vet, will check the kitten's health and bring her over here when she is a bit bigger and Sylvia will take over from my Morag who was a fixture here for years and I shared her with Bev when I was in Canada. I see no reason why it would not work just as easily as it did before."

Ashley knew there was no point in objecting. It was not her decision to make. She went off to bed with the hope that she could make good progress on the book before the distraction of a kitten stole away her aunt's attention to her memories of life with Lawren Drake.

※

The next morning Ashley's fears were realized. All Anna could talk about was what would need to be done before she could welcome Sylvia to her new home.

"The wee thing is living in a cardboard box at the moment. She will need a proper bed and a carrier cage to sleep in until we can trust her with free run of the house. Then there's her food to get and possibly a harness and lead for a time. Oh, and a litter tray of course. I think I should call Cameron and get him to run me into Oban. I can pick some things up at the vet's surgery and ask Callum Moir for advice about food, oh, and scratch boards to preserve our furnishings. And he will have to check the kitten over before he brings her home to us. Or more likely he will do that at Fiona's."

Anna looked across the empty breakfast dishes and thought her niece looked rather crestfallen at the sound of this plan.

"Of course, you should come too, Ashley. You were locked up here on your own all day yesterday. We could do some shopping and have lunch in town if you like. You never know, we might run into that nice Doctor Jansen and invite him to join us. What do you say?"

It would have been churlish to rebuke her aunt's enthusiasm so Ashley soon found herself clad in a warm coat against the cold west wind and settling into Cameron's Range Rover's back seat.

"I am hearing there's to be a new occupant at the estate house?" The question came from the driver as soon as the engine started.

"Now, I could ask how on earth you know that bit of information when I only found out about it myself yesterday, but it would be a silly question. You likely know more about everything that goes on within ten miles of this place better than anyone else."

Cameron chortled as he changed gears for the main road. "Ach, Mrs. Drake, it's nearer fifty miles than ten, I'm thinking. It was the vet who passed on the news to his assistant and she told her husband who mentioned it to ………."

"You can stop right there, Cameron. I get the picture."

Ashley suddenly came alive to this information situation. "So, Cameron, what did the town think about my Aunt Anna's adoption of the original Wildcat kitten?"

"Oh, that was in my dad's time as driver. He said it was a nine-day wonder with folks siding with Mrs. Anna or the vet at the first. Fiona was the go-between for that entire time and she said Anna Mason, as you were then, had won over the vet and got her a part-time job besides. It was clear the lady was respectful of the native species and it stood well in her stead in those early days, I can tell you.

Of course, our Fiona was one of your aunt's first contacts here and she is a supporter right to this very day."

Anna smiled in agreement with this summary and only the sound of wheels turning on the road surface was heard for a mile or so until Cameron resumed.

"Now I'm thinking about furry creatures, there was another story about Mr. Lawren and that cat Morag who followed when the wild one moved on to the animal sanctuary."

"Oh, and what was that about?" Ashley was determined to make the shopping expedition useful to her purposes in some way.

"If I remember it rightly from my dad's account, it was Fiona herself who saw something remarkable in the kitchen one day. Morag was a solitary wee thing. She did not like strangers over much but Fee saw her climb into Mr. Lawren's lap and purr like an engine while looking up into his eyes in a right peculiar way while he gently stroked her back.

Fee said it was quite unusual, but then, he was an unusual man, is that not so, Mrs. Drake?"

Anna swallowed a lump in her throat and replied quietly, "I can't argue with that, Cameron."

They rolled along in silence for a few minutes; each person lost in his or her own thoughts.

Cameron was thinking of his dad's years of driving and the many stories he told.

Ashley was making a mental note to include the cat stories in her book.

Anna was feeling the emotion that surfaced every time she heard someone refer to Lawren Drake and his incredible abilities. It was always a feeling compounded of loss and pleasure; loss that he was no longer by her side and pleasure that he was not forgotten by others.

The women decided to divide and conquer. The wind from the sea was carrying cold moisture that would soon develop into rain. Offshore, Kerrera Island was already disappearing under a cloak of cloud.

Ashley went to do the shopping while Anna headed to the vet's surgery to seek supplies.

It had been many years since she dared venture into the lair of the dragon, as she mentally named Callum Moir. It was a name derived from his decidedly brusque manner to all humans. He had given every evidence of greatly preferring the animal kingdom to the human one.

She found him busy with a large dog that had swallowed something nasty, but his receptionist directed her to the shelves where a variety of animal-related items were on display. She selected the main things she needed for Sylvia, then asked the receptionist about suitable foods.

"Oh, the vet will advise you about that Mrs. Drake. You will be needing a specialty food for a wild animal's digestion. Just take a seat for a minute. He should be finished shortly."

Anna sat down in the waiting room beside a woman with a tiny dog on her lap and a man holding firmly to the lead of a very large, very anxious, dog.

Callum Moir emerged from the consulting room removing rubber gloves from his hands and reporting first to the receptionist. She whispered to him that someone was waiting to speak with him and he turned in surprise to see Anna. She was also surprised to see him. It had been many years since their short and unsuccessful attempt at dating. She remembered him as abrupt of speech and dark of gaze but time seemed to have softened both elements. His hair was now completely silver although his eyebrows retained some of their original brown. He had always been tall and yet there was a slight stoop to his shoulders that could have been the result of a recent strenuous dog operation.

He reached out a hand to Anna and she thought there was a facial feature that had become more prominent if anything. His nose had always been rather large, narrowing at the bridge giving him a supercilious look. With age, this beak of a nose almost overpowered his face and Anna thought he looked even more ferocious. His voice, however, as he greeted her, had become mellowed and she saw a genuine smile light up his dark eyes.

"Anna, it has been too long. I heard you were back but then came the word you were very sick and confined to the house. I am glad to see you much improved and I think I can guess why you are here.

Excuse me for one minute. Please step into my office so we can talk."

He sent the woman with the tiny dog into the examining room and listened to the man's request for dental work for the large dog. Then he notified the receptionist to schedule an appointment and soon followed Anna into his small office.

Thus far, Anna had not been required to say anything in response. She decided to maintain her silence. Callum Moir seemed to have everything in hand.

"So, I take it you have been to see Fiona and decided to take the wildcat kitten?"

Straight to the point, as usual. Nothing changed there.

"You take it right, Doctor. I seem destined to rescue kittens in distress."

"Well, I am certain Fiona would have taken on the responsibility had she not a new bairn to look after."

"Oh, I am not complaining. Our time with Sylvester was cut short. It will be a treat to see this one to maturity, God Willing!"

"At the very least, you are familiar with the species, Anna, and with its peculiarities, to some degree.

I am more than willing to advise you if there are any difficulties."

"That is most kind of you, Callum. I don't recall you were quite this positive the last time."

He had the grace to blush slightly at the accusation and hemmed and hawed while he summoned a suitable response. "I plead guilty. I was considerably younger then. I hope experience has softened my approach somewhat."

"I am sure it has, as with all of us.

Now, I have set aside a number of items for Sylvia's comfort and safety. Could you glance over them and add anything you feel is needed?"

This task was soon done but the items had accumulated into a pile larger than Anna's shopping bag would contain. The vet offered to bring the bulky items when he conveyed Sylvia to her home in the estate farmhouse. Anna packed the rest into her bag, paid the bill and went on her way.

As she walked along the pavement, filled with jostling schoolchildren recently released from school, she wondered if Callum Moir's generosity regarding the kitten's supplies had been an excuse to contrive another meeting with the kitten's new owner.

For goodness sake, Anna Drake! You know better than that. He gave up on you decades ago, for good reason. The whole episode was not one of your finer moments.

Ashley Stanton was perusing the shelves of baked goods and trying to choose between chocolate eclairs with real cream, and a strawberry strudel. It would be nice to have an extravagant treat now the basic shopping was resting safely in her cart.

She reached out to take hold of both when she felt a tap on her shoulder.

"This is a nice surprise!"

Ashley quickly withdrew her hand and managed a crooked smile at Edmund Jansen, standing beside her with a bakery bag steaming gently in his hand.

"I often come here for a hot bridie," he explained. "It makes a change from sandwiches. My room has no cooking facilities."

"That's ridiculous! Where is this room, anyway?"

"Oh, it's above one of the shops on the High Street. I do have a kettle, however. Tea and instant coffee are always available should you wish to indulge."

Ashley felt an unexpected pang of sympathy for the young man. His living conditions did not sound ideal for someone in a responsible position. She guessed money was tight. On a sudden impulse, she responded.

" Well, I can offer you a home-cooked meal if you come to the farmhouse soon for that hill walk I promised you."

His eyes positively brightened at the thought. She was not sure if the food or the company was the attraction but, either way, he deserved something better to eat, once in a while, than a rapidly-cooling meat pie.

"I'll let you get home with your supper, Edmund. I have to pay for this lot. Phone when you have spare time and we'll do the climb."

He waved as she wound her way between browsing shoppers and headed for the checkouts.

Well I got myself into that, all right! I hope I bought enough to satisfy a hungry man.

Anna decided they should forgo a late lunch in Oban in favour of a meal at home with some of the fresh items Ashley already had in bags in her cart.

"I think we deserve a treat," said Anna. "I believe they still have delicious real, fresh cream eclairs here. It's something we can't get in Canada. Watch out for Cameron and I'll pop in and get them. The fast lane will let me through quickly."

Ashley sighed with satisfaction. Her Aunt Anna was in a good mood, supper was going to be easy with plenty to choose from and eclairs for dessert and there would be time afterwards for another chat about the book.

"Now that was delicious!" announced Ashley, as she wiped the last drop of cream and chocolate icing from her fingers. "Shall I make a pot of tea?"

"Certainly! Let's relax and you can ask me some more questions. I have been busy lately and I am sure you are getting impatient with me."

"Not at all, Aunt Anna, but you are right about the questions. I am still forming the shape of the book and I am wondering if you can remember any small incidents that defined Lawren for you. The kind of thing other people like to know about, if it's not too private of course."

Anna waited and tried to remember the type of incidents requested. Ashley had poured the tea and fetched her recording device before she had any ideas in mind. It was easier to remember the big events than to delve into the daily things that are significant at the time, although often relegated to the back of the mind thereafter.

"I will need time to think about this, Ashley. One thing does strike me though. Lawren always had a sketch book with him. He drew almost all the time for practice, I believe, and also because he was able to see things differently once he had committed them to paper."

"That's interesting. What sorts of things did he draw?"

"Many different things. I watched him capture tiny detail in a moss-covered stone wall or quickly outline the view of distant hills. He could not resist any statue we came across and would stand nearby and sketch it while people passed him and looked curiously at his page."

"What happened to his sketch books? I might get a cover picture for my book from one of Lawren's drawings."

"The majority of the sketch books were in his studio in Ontario and those went to Museum London for their

Local London Artists' collection. Now that I think of it, there might be one or two upstairs in the locked room above the porch. Take the key from the larder hook, Ash, and take a look for yourself. I will stay and enjoy another cup of this excellent tea. Let me know if you find anything useful."

Ashley did not need a second invitation. She was off up the stairs with key in hand. This was a great opportunity to see inside a private space in the house. She knew her aunt stored seasonal clothes in there but there might be more interesting items she had forgotten about.

The first sensation was a blast of fragrant air from the cedar wood planks lining the room. The clothes rail occupied the back wall and underneath she saw two suitcases and a number of boxes. One of these was open and held winter scarves, hats and gloves. The others had lids. On the wall opposite the door were shelves stacked with books and a few ornaments and also a tin can filled with an assortment of brushes and spatulas. She went immediately to these and picked out one or two, rubbing the handles as if she could sense the artist from these tools of his trade. This was a good sign. If brushes were here, there was a chance sketch books were here also.

She glanced along the shelves for something longer and slimmer than books but found nothing. Then she turned to the lidded boxes and in the second one she struck gold. Heavy art books weighed down the bottom. On top she found two large sketch books with Lawren's signature on the front and dates signifying their use over a period of three or four years.

She carefully flicked through the pages and was not surprised to see exactly what her aunt had described. Lawren Drake sketched everything he saw. Children at play on the beach, the hills of Mull emerging from the clouds, a sign above a shopfront, a beautiful, tinted rendition of Iona Abbey that caused Ashley to catch her breath and another completed drawing of three soldiers, labelled 'The Commando Monument.'

At once, she began to rethink the approach to her book. If she got permission to use some of these, it would elevate what had been a memoir to the level of a coffee table art book. The format would have to change to allow for full-page illustrations. This would mean a much more expensive production which her publisher would strenuously resist unless she could guarantee a readership with deep pockets.

A combination of anecdotes, personal revelations and never-before-seen artwork could bring in buyers both male and female.

Her excitement grew. Could the second sketch book reveal more spectacular finds? She could scarcely hope for more.

With trembling fingers she opened the pages and immediately saw that this folio was about the McCaig Estate Farmhouse. Morag slept peacefully on her window seat in several sketches and the painted bench outside was drawn in detail against the stone wall of the house with a pot of daffodils blooming at ground level. The wooden garage interior was featured, including a family of owls on a high rafter blinking in the light from the opened door, and a number of trees on the property at various seasons of the year were carefully rendered.

The second half of this sketch book was devoted to Anna. Ashley recognized preliminary drawings of the portrait that hung in the upper hall as well as Anna at work in the kitchen and in the garden. There was one compelling drawing of Anna asleep by the lounge fireplace with her book on her lap that seemed to shout Lawren's love for her in every delicate line.

Ashley slid down onto the floor under the south-facing dormer window with the sketches open on her knees. This was so much more than she could ever have hoped for. She was almost afraid to turn the pages to the last entry but again, she was astonished at her luck. At the very end was a self-portrait of Lawren Drake.

Could this be the only one he had ever done? If so, it had immense value, not only to Anna herself, but also to other artists and collectors.

As far as Ashley was concerned, at this moment, the value of these two sketch books lay in their immediate benefit to Anna's memory. If this exceptional collection could not stimulate her to recall incidents with Lawren, nothing could.

She was also keenly aware of the concomitant emotions these sketches might arouse in her aunt.

With the memories might come the sharp pain of loss. It was a delicate balance and Ashley Stanton, journalist and hopeful author, must find a way to level the balance of Anna Drake's emotions in her favour.

Chapter Fifteen

Ashley returned all her finds to their original places in the storage room and locked the door behind her.

It did not feel right to her to rush downstairs to the kitchen and regale her aunt with her exciting discoveries.

These sketches were private, especially the self-portrait. It would be best if Anna saw them on her own without her niece breathing down her neck with questions and comments.

This decision made, she was exceedingly glad to find Anna poring over her purchases for Sylvia and setting the supplies on a shelf in the larder. She seemed to have forgotten why Ashley had gone upstairs.

"What do you think? Should we set aside this top shelf for cat food? It's unlikely Sylvia would climb this high. The litter containers can be placed on the stone floor for now. Did I tell you the vet is going to deliver the heavier items when he collects Sylvia from Fiona's new house?"

"When do you expect that will be?"

"Oh, she's just a baby for now but much more sturdy than most kittens, of course. I'd say four weeks.

I hope it won't be longer. I do want to spend time with her before I need to go back to Canada."

"Did you have a return date in mind, Aunt Anna?"

"Well, I have an open ticket but I thought it would be nice to spend another Christmas here and go home after the New Year's rush is over. Will that work in with your own plans, Ashley?"

"My time is yours. I'll fit in with whatever you decide. I love it here now that my nursing duties are over."

"I do feel guilty about that. It was a huge imposition on your time, Ashley, and I apologize."

"Oh dear, I was not meaning to sound critical, Aunt Anna. It's just that the house and the garden and the surrounding area as well as the town, are much more available to me now. It's a very beautiful place."

The answer seemed to satisfy her aunt. She went back to stacking the shelf with cans and did not notice a frantic Ashley mentally counting the weeks until the New Year and revising her decision not to rush her aunt's memories.

She began the next morning over breakfast.

"Any special plans for today, Aunt Anna?"

"Only one and I am thinking you should come with me to Jeanette's house."

"Why?"

"Well, I think you need to see some of Lawren's best work on this side of the Atlantic. Jeanette and George commissioned a painting of their children; a family portrait. If we time it right, you will be able to compare the children today with his view of them several years ago when they were just small."

"That's an intriguing idea, Aunt Anna. Is Jeanette available?"

"She called last night. She's been bugging me to see her new house and advise about her arrangements for her mother Jean who's about my age. She wants to finalize the décor and facilities for Jean before she arrives from Vancouver to live permanently with the family."

"I'd be delighted to go with you but, if we are not in a rush, I need to tell you what happened when I went up to the storage room last evening."

Her aunt's face changed. She looked down at her plate and moved a few toast crumbs around with her finger. It was clear she was hesitating before answering.

"I do want to hear about your discoveries, Ashley, but first let me tell you something I remembered last night after I went to bed. It was Cameron talking about when Fiona saw Morag on Lawren's knee that tweaked my memory. I have to warn you, Ashley, it's a bit of a strange story."

"Go on. I won't think it strange."

"Well, I saw Morag on Lawren's knee several times and I, too, heard the purring. It was a deep, contented sound Morag never made with anyone else. Her quiet moments with me were never that blissful, I believe. The strange part of the story comes after Lawren was gone. Once or twice while I was here in the house and still in the dismal early stages of deep mourning, I heard that same, unmistakable purring sound coming from Morag.

When I looked at her, she was staring past me toward the stairs as if waiting for someone to come down into the kitchen to join us. I hardly breathed, it was such a peculiar sensation."

"What did you think?" Ashley's whisper was almost imperceptible. The hair on the back of her neck was standing up. Her hand went to the recorder in her pants' pocket and she quickly pressed the record button.

"I didn't know what to think at first, but in time I had to conclude the cat thought she saw Lawren again."

"Oh, my goodness! That is extraordinary. Did it always happen right here?"

"No, the last time was upstairs in my bedroom. I don't know if I should be telling you this, Ashley."

Oh, please do! Tell me, whatever it is!

A shiver of excitement went through her in anticipation of what was to be revealed.

"You see, I was having trouble sleeping and I brought Morag upstairs with me for company. She would curl up beside me on the pillow that was Lawren's, and sleep so soundly all night that I often was lulled back to sleep just because she was there as a comforting presence.

It was the deep purring noise that woke me in the middle of the night. Morag was sitting upright on the pillow and then she jumped down and moved over to the chair by the fireside as if someone else had come to claim his rightful place in the bed."

Ashley's sharp intake of breath was the only sound in the kitchen other than the ticking of a wall clock.

"All of that would be remarkable enough, but I have to be truthful, now that I have gone this far.

I was watching Morag in the dim light from the window when I swear I felt Lawren's hand on my cheek.

Of course, I could have been dreaming. And yet, I could feel the cool metal of his ring against my warm cheek. He used to gently touch my face with the back of his hand when he went out to walk on his own with his sketch book. It was a farewell signal; a very loving touch."

She paused for a second, then continued.

"I never again heard that purring or felt as if Lawren might be in the room with me.

That was the last time."

Ashley Stanton had no idea how to respond to her aunt's story. She watched in silence as a wave of emotions passed across the face she now knew very well. There was no doubting the sincerity of her aunt's memory. She believed every word she had said. It was more than likely no one, other than Ashley, had heard about this incident. It was another to add to the dream conversations Ashley had overheard when her aunt was so ill.

It was a privilege to be Anna Drake's confidante but the responsibility it brought with it was beginning to be a huge weight on her great-niece's mind.

. . .

Silence fell in the kitchen. Anna looked as if her thoughts were a million miles away.

Ashley fingered the recorder button in her pocket and prayed it had worked. The entire incident had been so amazing that she needed to quote it verbatim, if she ever did use it.

After a long three minutes, Anna seemed to come back to the present. She gave herself a shake and turned her attention to Ashley again.

"Now, what were you going to tell me about your visit to the storage room?"

Immediately, Ashley was presented with a dilemma. Did she dare expose her aunt to another emotional moment so soon after what had just happened? She made a quick decision to delay revealing the sketch book until later in the day.

"I think I will tell you about that later, Aunt Anna. When will we be going to Jeanette's house?"

"She will collect us and then go into town to pick up the children from school so you will be able to compare the portrait with the real subjects. We'll have tea with the family. Also, I want to have a word with George when he comes home."

"That sounds fine. I can do some work on the computer before that, if it's all right?"

"Of course it is. I will call Alina today. She will be anxious to find out how we have been managing here and I also need to do some clearing up in the garden before the weather changes. Oh, don't worry, Ashley. I will take it slowly and come back inside if I feel at all tired."

"Good! I can watch you from the office window so I'll know if you misbehave."

Anna laughed. "That word was one frequently applied to your grandfather Simon when we were young. I think you must have learned it from him, unless your mother adopted it also."

"I think everyone in the family used it in preference to saying outright that something or someone was behaving badly. It's not a word I ever gave any thought to before. I suppose it's one of those family habits that get passed down."

"It brought back good memories for me just then. Let's go about our business for now and we can reassemble for a late lunch before Jeanette appears. You know what a whirlwind she is. We should probably take a preventive nap to prepare ourselves."

The sad and spooky feelings seemed to have been dispersed by their shared laughter.

Ashley retired to the office with her recorder. She had last night's events to note and she must transcribe on the laptop, exactly what had been said this morning.

Anna went upstairs to dress for the outdoors and plan what she would say to Alina. She knew she must reassure her that strength and appetite were returning after the illness but she had the news about Fiona's baby, the new kitten, and the incredible eco house to relate. However, it might be advisable to delay telling Alina about her plan to stay in Scotland until after the New Year.

She glanced out of the window at the garden. The climbing rose needed to be tied up. The raised herb beds should be weeded and she must check on the peat and wood supplies in the shed. Although the weather had remained fairly mild, it was likely to change at a moment's notice. Better to get ahead with outdoor tasks now and be inside and cozy once the cold weather started. It occurred to her that she had once enjoyed doing these tasks with Lawren and now she was on her own. With the thought came a sense of gratitude for Ashley's continued presence. She would not feel safe living here on her own. The bout of illness had taught her that she was not invincible.

Time and age were creeping along and a sensible woman had to adjust to both.

❧

"Now, don't you be trying to compare our new place to Fiona and Gordon's. They could not be more different out there in the wilds of their estate. We are happy living in Oban town. It's easier for George, for my clients, and for the children's school."

" Mummy, Fergus Campbell did a talk today at school about their new house. It's really cool. The teacher called it a house of the future and she said we would all be doing energy saving things in our houses soon. What are *we* doing, Mummy?"

Jeanette turned to Liam and poured him more milk. "Well, we put more insulation in the roof, we have a high functioning furnace and we used automatic closers on the doors so you and your sister won't let the heat out when you go upstairs. Is that good enough for you, young man?"

"It's a start, I think. Can we go to see Fergus' house some day?"

"Perhaps we ca go in the summer, when the baby is bigger."

The promise seemed to satisfy Liam for the time being. He turned his head quickly to his plate and a fair curl tumbled forward onto his forehead.

He is more like his father every time I see him and he has his father's intelligence too.

His sister Annette was not listening to their conversation. She was cuddled up beside her namesake, sharing secrets. As far as she was concerned, she never got to spend enough time with her mother's friend who zoomed off to Canada again just as they were getting comfortable with each other.

"So, can I help look after Sylvia for you when you go home?"

"Why don't you ask your mummy to bring you over to the farmhouse whenever she comes to inspect my property. If Sylvia is at Auntie Bev's house, you can see her there and stay until your mother is finished with her work."

"Is that a promise?"

"I'll set it up with your mother, don't worry, my dear one."

"Goodie!"

Annette returned to the plate of sugar-free cookies set out for the children's after-school snack. She did not notice her mother and Aunt Anna's niece had left the room. It was comfortable to be close to Aunt Anna and have her attention. She wondered if it would be like this when her grandmother arrived from Vancouver to stay. There was something especially nice about older people. They were not in so much of a rush all the time.

"The painting is in the upstairs sitting room. As you've just seen the children you will be better able to judge its special qualities."

She entered a bright, cheerful room with two large windows and a fireplace flanked by bookshelves.

A craft table was covered with drawings, crayons and stickers and woven rugs decorated the floor over wide wooden floorboards.

It was the very definition of a family room and the large painting graced the opposite wall to the windows and benefited from the cool northern light.

Ashley stood back and marvelled at the artist's skill. Annette was a small child on her mother's knee while Liam stood proudly in front of his father. Each child looked at the same time, both young and older. It seemed to be something about their expressions. Lawren Drake had a caught a hint of Annette's spark of lively humour and of Liam's intelligent, inquiring mind. Ashley thought if the children's bodies were shown as they now looked, their original faces might be superimposed there without too much of a contrast.

She looked again at Jeanette who had moved to tidy the pencils scattered across the craft table. Her dark brown hair was longer than in the family portrait but it was easy to recognize the woman who sat so happily with her family. Any minor changes to her appearance had been predicted by Lawren Drake so that it looked like a contemporary work of art.

How had he managed to do this? Years had passed since the original portrait had been commissioned and yet, he had seen into the future in some mysterious way. Ashley could not judge if George McLennan's figure was similarly futuristic as she had not previously met him. She wondered if there were other examples of Lawren's art work in the town and if they all had the same characteristics.

When they returned to the kitchen, Anna had disappeared for a conference with her lawyer and Ashley helped Jeanette to prepare a high tea for the group. The children were sent off to their rooms to do homework and Ashley took the chance to ask Jeanette her opinion about Anna's deceased husband.

"So you saw the amazing portrait painting? I thought you would be impressed. We think it is prescient as do most people who have seen it. Anna's husband was a remarkable man in many ways. It's to her credit that Anna acknowledged his unusual characteristics and was not put off by them."

Ashley continued to arrange small iced cakes around a platter and asked, "What do you mean by unusual characteristics?"

Jeanette sliced sandwiches into triangles and licked her fingers before replying.

"It's hard to describe. He had a way of looking at you as if he saw inside your heart and liked what he saw there. It gave you a glad feeling and made you smile back at him. He never said much. He was an observer more than a talker but when he did make a comment it was always worth listening to.

George and I liked him a lot even although we had our suspicions at the start of their relationship.

We were wary he might hurt her in some way because he was so different. Anna, of course, adored him. They were like two halves of a beautiful object; each special in its own way but when placed together they were ten times more admirable."

It was another quote worthy of remembering.

"How was she after he died?"

"Bev and I were able to support her then. Alina came over from Canada to join us but for weeks she was inconsolable. It was the suddenness of his passing. None of us was prepared. He was too young to die. It was very hard for Anna to take."

"I know Lawren died in Scotland but in Canada we were so upset for Anna that I never did hear about the details of his death. What did you know?"

Jeanette turned away to wash her hands and Ashley could not see her expression until she chose to face her again.

"Anna has never talked about it to any of us. We never dared introduce the subject after she had eventually got over it enough to carry on again. All I ever knew was that they were alone when it happened. Were you intending to include this kind of personal stuff in your book?"

"Honestly, I am not sure yet what will be included. I am merely collecting information at this stage.

I need to get a picture of this man who was so important to Anna and whose art work has such an effect on everyone who admires him. The big decisions will come later with my Aunt Anna's approval of course."

"I am glad to hear that, Ashley. Quite frankly, between us as fellow Canucks, several of Anna's long-time friends are surprised she agreed to the book project in the first place."

"Yes, I got that impression."

"There is one advantage to the idea."

"Please tell me."

"If, as it seems, Anna is ready to reveal her feelings about

Lawren to the world, it indicates she is ready to move ahead again with her life."

Ashley heaved a big sigh. "I do hope you are right, and that my book will help in some way. There will be more attention to them as a couple, at first, but if she is ready for it, the end result will be something that will live on after she is gone."

"A kind of immortality I suppose?"

"Hopefully, it will be."

※

"So, Anna, what can I do for you? It's so good to see you looking like your old self."

George took a breath and began again. "Wait! That didn't sound right. My wife is always telling me to be careful what I say to women about their appearance. I didn't mean to indicate you look old, Anna."

"Oh George, we know each other well enough so that you never need to apologize to me for anything.

I know how good your heart is. None better." He gulped at the compliment.

She collected a pile of folders from the chair opposite George's messy desk and found a place for them on top of a filing cabinet.

"Apologies for the mess! Jeanette insisted on me bringing my current files here. I think she has the idea it will keep me at home more, but I still need some time to arrange the study as an efficient office. I'm afraid it will lead to duplication of files. There's nothing more annoying than to come home to do some work and discover the very thing I need the most is still in Oban."

Anna laughed. George was always in a mess but it never stopped him from finding a required document or giving the best possible advice to his clients. He had been invaluable to her even before she left London, Ontario, on her way to Scotland to solve the mysterious legacy of the McCaig Estate Farmhouse.

"George McLennan, I am sure you will settle in quickly in your fine new residence, and provide your usual exemplary service to all and sundry."

She made herself comfortable on the vacated armchair and looked across the desk to see if George had changed at all since he now had two children, a busy wife with a thriving business, and a new, larger home further up the hill above the town. She noticed a grey hair or two on his fair head and thought his hairline was gradually moving backward, but his eyes were full of concern for his client and his smile was as genuine as ever.

"I'll cut to the chase before Jeanette calls us downstairs for tea.

You know I have been ill for some weeks? I am feeling much better now and it seems to me it is time to think ahead. I know only too well how suddenly life can end and I am anxious to settle some matters for my peace of mind."

"Of course, Anna."

He pulled together a legal pad and a pen and looked serious and ready to take notes.

"I want my great-niece Ashley Stanton to inherit the Oban house after I die. She is pursuing a very uncertain profession and her mother is of no real use to her as far as support is concerned. Donna is not in a secure position herself and I doubt Ashley will ever be able to rely on her help.

The girl has shown a real concern for the old house, and for me, and she loves the countryside. I think she would be happy here."

He made some notes, then asked if there was anything further she wanted.

"I do have a number of bequests to outline. Donations to local charities and the like, but the bulk of my estate will be left to Fiona for her family, and to Bev for her children and grandchildren, and to Jeanette and to you, George, for the two children, or more children, if you decide to have them."

"Ah, as I am a beneficiary of your will, I need to consult a colleague who will meet with you, once I have drawn up the provisions as you requested. There must not be any hint of undue influence on my part with regard to these bequests."

"Whatever you say, George. There is one more thing I want to ensure."

He raised his pen again and waited attentively.

"You will surely remember, how useful my local knitters' group has been in the success of the A plus Company. I would like to set aside a significant sum of money, under your control, to maintain the knitting project and to encourage younger women, and men, to continue the longstanding customs of unique craftwork that exist in this part of Scotland."

He sat back in his chair and swiveled around for a second while he was gathering his thoughts.

"Do you mean something like a Knitters' Co-operative Company?"

"That is exactly what I want, George, if you don't object to the extra work this will bring?"

"Not at all! It is an excellent idea. But, if I may, Anna, I must ask what provisions you have made for your friend Alina regarding the A Plus business in Canada?"

"You need have no concerns about that matter, George. In fact, I spoke to Alina earlier today and she assures me the online business is booming. Her latest idea is to add step-by-step videos to the website so young people can learn how to knit and crochet. It is generally accepted that knitting is a therapeutic activity for all ages.

In any case, all matters pertaining to the online company will be settled separately in Canada with a portion of the profits automatically sent to you for the projects we have discussed."

"Well, Anna, I trust we shall not need to implement your

instructions for a long, long time but I will draw up the details and you can inspect the documents whenever you wish."

"Thank you, George. I knew I could rely on you, as I always have done."

He cleared his throat on hearing her commendation. He was not one for overt affection but Anna Mason Drake was a special person, as she had just demonstrated.

He contented himself with a hearty, "Let's go down for tea before those two young gannets have scoffed every sandwich and cake in the place!"

Chapter Sixteen

The phone rang just after breakfast had been cleared away. The interruption came just at the point where Ashley was wondering how to introduce the subject of Lawren Drake's sketch books.

"It's for you, Ashley"

"Who would be calling me?"

Anna Drake just smiled and handed her the phone.

"I was wondering if you were free this afternoon? I have a few hours off but Dr. Williams is taking a holiday starting tomorrow and so this may be my last chance to see you for some time."

"Oh, Edmund!" She thought quickly. "I guess that would be all right. I seem to remember I promised you a meal. Would you like to take a walk to the top of the hill first and then we can eat after we have worked up an appetite?"

She knew she was rushing along with the offer when she had no idea what she was going to cook and a schedule of work she had intended to do, but it seemed unkind to refuse the doctor an opportunity for a decent meal and some exercise in the fresh air.

"That's uncommonly generous of you, Ashley. I am

looking forward to seeing you later. About two o'clock, if that's convenient."

"Absolutely! See you then…………… and Edmund, wear your climbing boots!"

"I'll do that. Bye!"

He was gone and she had now two new items in what had been already, a full agenda.

She reported her plans to Anna and received an unexpected comment.

"I've been thinking about the young doctor's living accommodations. It does not seem right that he works so hard for the town and has little or no amenities on his down time. Would you like me to ask Fiona if her house in town is currently rented?"

"Does she have a house of her own as well as the castle and the new eco house? She *is* a rich woman!"

"Well, she was not rich at all originally. She inherited her small stone cottage near the seafront when her Granny died. It's rented out to holidaymakers mostly, but it has tiny rooms, all with basic furnishings.

In case you got the wrong idea about Fiona, you should understand I have never known anyone more hardworking than she is. She supported herself by working two jobs from a very young age as her Granny was the only family she had. She may seem like the fine Lady of the Castle now, but I can assure you, Gordon Campbell is the lucky one in that partnership. She will keep his feet on the ground no matter what happens."

"I can see you have great respect for Fiona, Aunt Anna, and I think your idea is a brilliant one for Edmund Jansen. I won't say a word about this today, of course. If it works out for him, I'm sure he will be delighted."

"Good. Now, let's see if we can squeeze in some book material into what is becoming a busy day for you. What did you find upstairs in the storage closet?"

Ashley's heart began to beat faster. This was the tricky part.

"Well, I think you should check it out for yourself. You will be surprised and I hope pleased, with your discoveries. As you suspected there are several of Lawren Drake's sketch books up there.

I'll get ahead with preparation for a meal for three while you investigate."

"Sounds intriguing! Go ahead, Ashley. There's a pork roast in the larder and the last apples from the tree for applesauce or apple crumble if you feel ambitious. Edmund Jansen looks like he could use a good meal for a change. Don't tire him out on the climb."

By one o'clock, Ashley had seasoned the pork and prepared applesauce. She thought custard poured over pound cake and jam would be a filling dessert and she set the sliced cake out in dishes. She also made a timetable for Anna of when the roast should go in the oven and added a reminder to leave enough milk for custard. After the domestic chores were done she had headed to the office. She was just about to solve the preliminary organization of the proposed book's contents and she needed an hour's work on that before Edmund arrived.

The one thing she forgot to do, was to check on her aunt.

The result of this omission was that Ashley was upstairs dressing for a hike when Edmund Jansen arrived and she suddenly remembered she had no clue what her aunt's reaction to the sketches was. It would have to wait until later.

They set off up Helen's Hill in good spirits despite a final warning from Anna to watch the weather.

Ashley was annoyed that she had not had time to listen to the radio weather report but she looked up to the top of the hill and estimated they could be up and back before any serious change occurred.

Edmund puffed a little as they reached the last section. He declared he must be out of shape as he was no stranger to climbing on the east coast.

"I am more of rock scrambler, I confess. Going over cliffs and down to the sea is more my speed but looking out to sea never gave me views like these. You can't tell until you get to the top that the mountains connect up like this and run for miles in all directions. How far can you actually go?"

"I'm afraid I don't know the answer, Edmund. I believe going west from here is how you can get to Bev and Alan Matthews' place. It's not too far."

"Could we try that? You could tell me the history of Helen's Hill on the way."

It seemed like a simple plan. They passed by the deep tarn, full of water from the recent rains and Ashley pointed out the rock formation that was a favourite place for climbers to rest.

"Helen Dunlop, or Fraser, or whatever one of her many names you prefer, was the woman who bought this property including the hill we are on.

She lived here alone for many years and few people in Oban knew much about her. She was a private person for reasons Anna Mason only discovered after years of investigations."

"So there must have been a relationship between your aunt and this Helen?"

"Yes, but it was far in the past, I believe. In any case it was a tragic story and Helen gifted the house and property to her only surviving female family member in Canada."

"I am guessing that was your Aunt Anna?"

"Right!"

"It was a wonderful gift."

"Indeed it was! You wouldn't know it now, but at that time, Anna Mason was a far different person with a life in

Canada that had not gone the way she had hoped. My grandfather, Anna's brother Simon, told me she gained a whole new perspective on life when she decided to keep the Estate Farmhouse.

It wasn't an easy decision for her, but it was the right one as it has benefited so many other people."

They continued in a westerly direction for some minutes, clambering over tufts of thick grass and skirting the huge rocks that had landed on this level from some unseen higher elevation.

Ashley soon realized she had gone farther than she had intended as the knoll that was the top of Helen's Hill vanished from view. With a breath of relief she stepped carefully to the top of a rise from which she could look down on the farmhouse of Bev and Alan Matthews. She continued her story.

"One example of people who are glad Anna came here, is down there in the valley. Bev was one of Aunt Anna's friends who arrived in Scotland to visit and fell in love with local sheep farmer Alan. His mother looked after Anna once when she had flu, much the same way I looked after her recently.

Watch where your feet go, Edmund, and you can see their farmhouse. Bev bakes and serves a farmhouse-style tea to holiday makers in the summer months.

They were poised on the rise looking downward and counting the sheep racing about on the hillside, when a sudden gust of wind swept upward from the valley and pushed against them with unexpected force.

"Wow! That's a strong wind," said Edmund, as he grabbed Ashley's arm and pulled her to safety.

All at once, Ashley became aware that while they were talking and walking along with their heads down because of the rough ground under their feet, the clouds above them had gathered together with frightening speed and what had been a grey day had now turned to menacing dark storm clouds descending around them and blocking out the light.

Before she could state the obvious, the situation became much worse. As the light disappeared, the icy rain began to pour down from the banks of roiling clouds and they were almost immediately soaked to the skin. What was worse was the effect the clouds were having as they pressed onto the mountain tops. She could not see further than a few yards back the way they had come.

Ashley was shocked into silence, but Edmund was more used to emergency situations and he recovered first. "Do you think we can retrace our steps back to Helen's Hill?"

Ashley looked around her again, and saw visibility was rapidly decreasing in all directions with the possible exception of the descent into the valley that led to the Matthews' farmhouse.

"I don't think we have any choice. I should have been watching the weather. The rain will make the journey down this valley dangerous, Edmund, but I can't see another way. We'll freeze if we stay up here and as we go down there might be more shelter."

"No worries! I'll lead the way. Remember I told you about my cliff climbing days? This is more like the conditions I was used to on the east coast. Tie your headscarf tightly and pull up your coat collar. We'll need to watch for slippery conditions underfoot but stay close and we'll make it."

It was twenty minutes Ashley would never forget. They scrambled over the edge and were met with boulders of various sizes that seemed to be vying for the chance to trip up their feet. The knowledge that a wrenched ankle would be, not only painful but also dangerous, made Ashley tense up until she could feel cramp in her calves at every step. Edmund went ahead and reached back his hand for her whenever he saw a difficult section. She leaned against his shoulder gratefully and took in deep breaths, only then realizing she had been holding her breath in fear.

Her headscarf soon provided no protection as the rain just dripped from it into her eyes. She relied on Edmund's tall figure and the surefooted way he tested larger rocks for stability before leading her ever downward, step by step. It was slow and laborious progress.

When they finally arrived onto the upper reaches of a steep meadow, Ashley could hardly see ahead. The mist from the clouds had followed them. The next problem came from their sodden footwear that had gripped onto the rocks but could not manage the grass of the meadow in its slippery state.

Edmund threw caution to the winds, plopped himself down onto the grass and proceeded to slide downhill for all the world like some school kid on a plastic tray.

Ashley saw no other option.ABandoning her only overcoat to its fate she grabbed its sides and stuck her feet out in front and followed her companion's example. Several sheep, on their way to more sheltered areas, jumped aside in alarm as the pair slid by at increasing speeds.

Fortunately, Alan Matthews was watching the sheep out of his kitchen door's glass panel and saw the unusual sight of two people tobogganing down his field in a rainstorm. He called to his wife to get blankets and hot drinks. Then he donned his long waterproof coat and wide-brimmed hat and grabbed his hiking poles from the tall jar by the door before heading out as fast as he could into the fierce wind.

He knew there was a fenced area near the farmhouse which the two people could not see from their position. If they struck the fence at the speed they were going there would be an accident.

Possibly a serious one.

Calling the strangers all kinds of rude names under his breath, he made his way with the help of the poles, to a spot near the fencing where the two 'idiots' might see his signal to stop or turn aside.

Edmund was in the lead, with Ashley fast approaching, when he realized what was happening.

By applying brute strength he turned his moving body around to present a broadside barrier into which Ashley, feet first, soon crashed with an impact that stopped her progress but set Edmund rolling out of control.

Alan had seen the manoeuvre and he bent down to grab the rolling figure. He had thought the two were teens, or even children. He could not imagine who else would be so crazy as to risk life and limb in such a stupid way, but he quickly saw the man and woman were adults. They were both covered from head to foot in mud, their clothes were ruined, the female had lost a shoe and the man had been knocked dizzy by the impact of her body.

His every instinct urged him to rail at the pair for their stupidity but he held his peace for the time being. The first task was to get them out of the weather and into warmth as soon as possible. The girl's teeth were chattering and her hair was dripping all over her face.

He lifted up the young man, gave him the hiking poles for support and picked the girl up in his arms.

"Follow me as fast as you can!"

In mere minutes the trio was falling into the farmhouse kitchen where Bev awaited them with towels, blankets, spare clothes, a steaming kettle and soft words. She gave her husband a cautionary look that said, "Not now, Alan!" and took the girl into the bathroom, leaving the men to sort themselves out at the kitchen sink.

When Bev emerged some minutes later with Ashley Stanton by her side wrapped in a voluminous dressing gown, it was her look of astonishment that calmed her husband down.

"Alan, this is Anna's niece Ashley who has been staying at the estate house, and the young man with his head under the tap in the sink, is the new Oban doctor, Edmund Jansen."

That was enough to shock Alan Matthews into silence. He

waited until the doctor had squeezed the worst of the water out of his hair and dried his face. Edmund was now dressed in a pair of Alan's working dungarees fastened around his slender waist with a large leather belt. The wool sweater was also too large but its warmth was more than welcome.

"Well now, come over to the fire and sit down. Hot tea and scones will be ready in a second and then you can tell us what happened." She glared at Alan in case he should countermand her orders.

Ashley asked if she could first phone her aunt to reassure her of their safety.

"She will be worried sick knowing where we were heading. She absolutely must *not* attempt to climb Helen's Hill to rescue us."

"I'll do that for you, Ashley. Help Alan to set the small table by the fire and get the hot food into you.

You'll both feel better soon, although your young man here will have some mighty big bruises for a while if I'm any judge of such things."

There was a strained silence as Ashley did as requested. She and Edmund could not look each other in the face but they fell upon the raisin and cheese scones as if they had not had a chance to eat for days and soon demolished the plateful, washing them down with copious draughts of hot tea while thawing their stockinged feet at the blazing fire.

When Bev returned from phoning, it was to inform them that Anna was greatly relieved to hear they were safe and she insisted Bev and Alan return the pair to the estate house along with what could be saved of their clothing and everyone should stay for a meal until the weather had calmed down.

Edmund tried to refuse the offer of hospitality but Ashley would not hear of it.

"You probably saved my life, Dr. Jansen, and my aunt will be anxious to thank you in person."

Their shoes were ruined so they went out to the big Land

Rover in wellington boots and with their other wet and muddy clothes in a garbage bag. It was a short ride to the estate house but already the track off the main road was awash in mud and icy running water.

Anna met them on the path to the garage with a golf umbrella and she hustled them indoors quickly, exclaiming at the state of them. She had to try to stifle her desire to laugh outright. Ashley and Edmund looked like two bedraggled dogs, heads hung low from a serious scolding.

She sent Ashley upstairs to change and offered Edmund more suitable clothing from a chest of Lawren's clothes she had retrieved from the storage cupboard when Bev had told her on the phone what kind of state the two were in.

As soon as the young people disappeared upstairs to sort themselves out the three friends dissolved in laughter.

"Have you ever seen anything like that?" exclaimed Alan after he had given an outline to Anna.

"I am glad I saw what happened," returned Bev. "No one would believe it otherwise. Neither James nor Eric ever got up to such antics when they were here. This will be a story to tell for decades!"

"Oh, don't be too hard on them, Bev. I am sure a few lessons have been learned. The good doctor will feel better once he hears my news, after we've eaten every bite of this meal, of course.

Alan, pour the whisky please. The plates are warming."

"Anna, the food smells wonderful. This reminds me of when we all used to gather in the kitchen for food, talk and laughter. We had some grand times here in the old days."

"Well, Alan, let's call it the *new* days and enjoy every minute we can together. I found something amazing earlier today and I will share it with you later."

"It's going to be a party!" said Bev, clapping her hands with delight.

Chapter Seventeen

It did seem like a party once Ashley had changed and dried her hair. She had a moment of shock when she saw Edmund sitting on the window seat wearing borrowed casual clothes that reminded her of Lawren. She wondered if her Aunt Anna had also seen the resemblance, but that lady was busy setting out plates of steaming vegetables beside a platter of sliced pork and a bowl of fragrant applesauce.

Alan insisted on a toast to the intrepid climbers and as the amber liquid slid down her throat Ashley felt a glow of warmth inside to match the outward comfort of being safe, warm and dry again.

Edmund was quietly watching as the older people exchanged stories of other events around the big farmhouse table. Anna informed Bev about the new wildcat kitten's arrival and saw her delight.

"I never realized how much I missed that wee furry Morag until she was gone. It will be good to have another one around when you are back in Canada, Anna. It's not a real home without a cat."

"Ah, speaking of a real home, I have news for *you*, Dr. Jansen."

Ashley looked up from her custard and cake in surprise. How had Anna accomplished this so fast?

"You will soon be able to recover from your bruised ribs, young man, in a comfortable bed in your new rental accommodations, thanks to Fiona Campbell."

"What? How did this happen? Didn't we visit the Campbell castle recently?"

"Fiona is a dear friend of mine and she has a charming little cottage by the seashore where you can stay as long as you like, or until next summer's holiday makers arrive."

"But, that sounds wonderful! Thank you so much. I can't believe how kind you are, Mrs. Drake, to arrange this for me, especially after I almost killed your great-niece here."

"Wait just a minute," objected Ashley, "I am not so fragile, you know. I should be apologizing to you, Edmund, for not keeping an eye out for the changing weather conditions."

"Never mind," insisted Alan. "It's a lesson learned, and given the circumstances, it was a bold move to slide down the field like that. Although, I'm thinking some of the sheep will never recover from the shock!"

That set them all off into gales of laughter and all tension immediately evaporated from the warm kitchen.

It was much later, after the table had been cleared and the brown betty teapot refilled, that Anna remembered her other discovery.

"Before you two head off for home and the doctor climbs back in his car, I have another surprise.

Edmund, if I may call you by your first name, this will not mean much to you, but bear with me. Ashley pointed me in the direction of an amazing discovery that is an incredible link to my past. Unknown to me, several sketchbooks belonging to Lawren Drake were in a storage cupboard upstairs. The sketches mean so much to me because I can recall most of the times and places where they were created.

More important than that, however, is the self-portrait drawn by my husband. You see, he was always looking outward at other people and scenes, and he never allowed me to take photos of him. He was superstitious about it for some reason. I don't know when he did the work, but it is beyond comforting to me to have this drawing here. I have Ashley to thank, of course."

There were tears in her eyes as she fetched the sketch from the larder shelf where it had been waiting for this moment. She held it up so everyone could see it.

Edmund had no connection to the sketch but he saw the effect it had on the Matthews and on Anna herself.

Ashley felt happy her secret was out and her aunt had accepted the portrait sketch without any adverse comments. There was still a lot to decide about the sketches in general, and whether they could be an addition to the book, and yet, it seemed as if her aunt's attitude would be one of approval.

It had been a long, challenging day, but for Ashley Stanton it had brought her closer to the Matthews and to Edmund Jansen. The danger they had shared and survived, was a bond she thought would be maintained during the weeks remaining of her time in Scotland.

Two things were clear to her. She had plenty of work ahead and she must buy a new coat and shoes before the worst of the winter weather descended.

***

Overnight the wind dropped but snow covered the ground and drifted down from the mountain tops.

"This is the best kind of snow," declared Ashley, as she stood, wrapped in a tartan shawl, looking out from the office at the garden. "It's not too heavy and it lingers on the branches of trees like lace. Every bush and plant is outlined in white, at least until the wind returns."

"Well, I suppose we can't complain. It's been a long, autumn season and we are getting close to December." Anna gently pulled her great-niece's shawl up closer to her neck. She was concerned that the previous day's adventure might have resulted in a chill or cold. Ashley had eaten a huge bowl of porridge for breakfast, however, and seemed anxious to get back to work since the snow indicated resting at home was required.

"Right then, what do you want me to do next to help with the writing?"

Ashley returned to her seat behind the desk and looked at her aunt. "I think we have some great material already. With the possible addition of the sketches, we would move into an illustrated book and for that I need my publisher's approval. Meantime, I do have a gap in the story but I am reluctant to broach the subject, Aunt Anna."

"Surely we know one another well enough now! You can ask me anything. I said at the start that I am ready to let the world know more about my husband and I am not changing my mind."

Ashley rubbed her hands together before beginning. "This could be too personal. I would understand if you chose to keep it private."

"Tell me. Opening up memories has the ability to take the sting out of them no matter how private they have been."

"If you say so, and only if you are certain."

Ashley began in a very quiet voice to denote her respect for the one whose confidences were to be revealed. "As far as I can discover, none of your friends knows exactly how Lawren died."

There was an audible gasp from her aunt and Ashley feared she had gone too far. To her relief, Anna began to talk after a moment during which it seemed she was gathering her courage.

"I was expecting this question to arise at some point and I am pleased to be able to tell you about it, Ashley. It is a memory that has been hidden away for long enough."

Anna Mason Drake settled herself in the spare padded chair beside the desk and looked out to the garden. Ashley pressed play on her recorder and waited, in high suspense.

"Ashley, your published interview was the one that told the world Lawren died of a sudden aneurism.

At the time, the loss was too near to me and I could not speak freely about it. I will tell you how and where he died and leave it to you how much you will share with the public.

It's difficult to imagine that day, with snow now covering all the details of the garden. It was high summer then, and we were out for a drive in the countryside around here. There are so many lovely spots and Lawren was always intrigued by the side roads and byways. He would say, 'Let's go down this way, Anna. Let's explore! Who knows what wonders we could uncover along the roadside or in a field?'

Of course, with this attitude and his uncanny sense of the unusual, we often did find a romantic ruined castle or a standing stone at a crossroads and he would begin a tale to match the circumstances while I just listened in amazement at his powers of invention.

If the scenery merited it, he would sit on a drystone wall and sketch while I gathered wildflowers. I kept a plastic bag filled with water in the car for such occasions. I looked up the names of the flowers, later, in the books Helen left here."

As she spoke, Anna's voice grew softer, younger, and more joyful and a smile lingered at the corner of her mouth. Ashley dared not interrupt but she hoped the voice recording would serve as a reminder, not only of the words, but also of the way her aunt looked at these moments.

"We had driven for some miles along a track that led higher into the mountains. I remember there was a stream running fast just to the left of the track and Lawren remarked on how brackish the water looked. I knew it came through the peat bogs under the mountains and tumbled over the rocks down to the sea. He said it must be the reason why whisky tasted so special in Scotland and I agreed.

It was a glorious, bright, warm day. Birds of prey were circling far above us on the thermals and heather was just beginning to set its buds for the Fall display.

The track we were on gradually became more narrow and it came to an end a mile or so further on.

A low wall of rough stones marked where a cottage had once stood. Lawren turned the car for the return journey then stopped the engine. The silence descended around us. A breeze blew in through the open car windows and I suddenly craved to be outside. Lawren followed me through the knee-high grasses and over to what must once have been a small garden around the long-deserted cottage. I spied a different variety of lavender growing between two rocks and stepped carefully over the debris to reach it.

Behind me, Lawren stood still and breathed deeply. He said, and I remember every word, for it was the last thing he ever said. 'This is a beautiful land, full of mystery and solitude but crying out with the voices of those who lived and loved among its mountains and wide spaces. I am so glad you brought me here, my dearest Anna. I have never felt so at peace in my entire life as I have with you in these glens and moors.'

I swiveled round to return his compliments and saw he had sunk to his knees amid the stones. At first, I thought he had spied some wild mushrooms or a beetle with an iridescent shell, but then he slowly collapsed and lay motionless.

I went to him at once and cradled his head in my lap. I knew he was gone. I felt his spirit leave. I sat there for however long I cannot tell, weeping, and talking to him about how happy he made me, recalling our life together and the sweet moments we shared.

It did not occur to me that I needed to summon help until

the sky began to darken and I felt a chill that was much deeper than the shiver of my skin.

In the end I removed my cardigan and made a pillow for his head. I could scarcely think but I knew I did not want an ambulance to come screeching along the track with harsh voices asking me questions, so I called Grant. He sensed by the tone of my voice that something significant had happened. All he asked for were what I saw around me and where we had left the main road. I told him what I could and I kept my phone open so he could get updates as he grew closer. Grant knew the country well. Only he could have found us. It was the old cottage at the end of the track that gave him the clue.

Together we carried Lawren to the back seat of his car and I sat beside my love as we went back to Oban. Grant called the doctor on the way and alerted Bev and Alan to be there at the house with lights on and a stiff drink waiting for me.

I really can't remember anything else, Ashley. The shock finally hit and I collapsed for some days."

There was a long silence after this. The stillness outside the office window mirrored the stillness inside the room. Ashley hardly dared to breathe. She was astounded at her aunt's courage. She did not intend to ask more but the quiet voice continued once again.

"Lawren was buried on Iona on a plot of land belonging to an ancient church on the island, near The Bay At the Back of the Ocean where we had been so happy together. As much of this as possible was kept secret. Only a few people know where he lies. It is not likely anyone would find his grave accidently.

I marked the spot in such a way that it is not obvious to the casual walker.

I sometimes return to Iona and visit the Abbey where we married. Then I walk across the island to his burial place.

The entire island of Iona is a place of pilgrimage so it is fitting that he rests there within hearing of the sea. Lawren Drake was a pilgrim voyager of sorts from his beginning to his end. I was privileged to join him on part of his journey.

I choose to believe his heart failed at a moment of extreme happiness."

Ashley gulped. She was overcome with emotion and reached out a trembling hand to touch her aunt's hands as they lay folded in her lap. On feeling the sympathetic touch, Anna Drake turned at last from the window view and smiled at her niece.

"It's all right, Ashley dear. I feel lighter now that I have told the story to you. It was a hard experience but time has softened its impact and now I am at peace with it.

I'll leave you here to work, if that's what you want. I will go back upstairs and look over the rest of what is stored in the cedar closet. There may be more items you can use for the book."

Ashley watched her go but she did not feel like working. The entire episode had left her exhausted.

She was beginning to get a real understanding of who Lawren Drake was as an extraordinary man, a consummate artist and a loving husband.

This knowledge came with an accompanying fear that she would not be capable of doing justice to him.

She hoped it was a temporary weakness. She sensed that if the author cannot have faith in her project the reader will also lose faith in her efforts.

Pulling the shawl closer to her neck, she closed up her notebook and switched off the recorder.

Her cell phone was lying on the desk and she decided to phone Edmund to see how he was doing after the previous day's adventure. It would be a touch of normality in what was shaping up to be a highly dramatic day.

She reached him at once but soon found out just how busy he was.

"Hi Edmund! I'm just checking in to find out how your ribs are doing?"

"Oh, Ashley I was about to do the same thing for you but the surgery has been madness all morning. There have been several car accidents due to the sudden icy rain and subsequent snow conditions. Nothing too serious, I'm glad to say. Cuts and bruises mainly. Doc Williams got away safely on the train to Glasgow, so I am on my own here."

"Sorry! I won't keep you. Call me later if you can."

"No wait! Please pass on my thanks to your aunt. I had a visit this morning from Fiona Campbell. She said she had just delivered her children to school and thought I might like to inspect the cottage. She left the keys with me. Ashley, would you go with me this evening? I need a feminine perspective on what might be required. I could collect you around seven, if that's not too late?'

"Oh, sure, Edmund! I'd be happy to help. I'll see you later then."

"Wonderful!"

And he was gone.

Ashley had a thought that his ribs were not preventing him from working but he would not likely have time to eat in such a busy day. She was keen to see the cottage by the shoreline and she would make up a picnic basket they could share in his new home. She went at once to the kitchen to see what she could make into sandwiches. A flask of hot soup would be tasty and she could include cookies and teabags in case the cottage kitchen was not stocked. That led her to the problem of how to transport milk so she went into the larder to look for a jar with a secure lid. Once everything was assembled she realized she would need to borrow a coat from her Aunt Anna for the evening expedition.

Anna was upstairs in the storage closet and she quickly extracted a winter coat and a pair of sturdy shoes for Ashley.

As she did so she concealed behind her back another item she had uncovered in her search.

"Oh, these smell wonderful! I would love to have a cedar-lined closet one day."

Anna looked on as her great-niece tried on the coat. In her mind was the knowledge that Ashley would inherit this very closet one day. It made her think of Helen Dunlop who likely stood in this same spot and may have thought of her distant relative possibly inheriting the estate house. The difference between the two incidents was that Helen never had the chance to know the woman to whom her house was offered. Neither did she know for sure that Anna Mason would accept the challenge of crossing the ocean and beginning a new life in Scotland. It was another reason why Anna felt blessed that she had such a close relationship with Ashley.

"Hmm!" she said, "you had better pack a torch and some candles. The electricity might not be on. It wouldn't matter during the day but it would be a problem at night. Look around when you get there, Ashley, and see if there's anything we can add for the doctor's comfort in the cottage. Sometimes an extra item or two makes all the difference although I'm sure Fiona has left the place in good order. After all, it was her childhood home and has many memories of her Granny."

"Good ideas! I'll do that. By the way, what happened to Fiona's parents?"

"Her father was a fisherman with his own boat. He drowned in a storm while Fiona was just a child and her mother died soon after from a broken heart, or so they say. It might have destroyed a lesser girl than Fiona but her Granny was a tough old Scotswoman and Fiona learned to be independent and to work hard. That's why I admire her so much. She has never changed in all the years I have known her. I am so glad she found true happiness with Gordon Campbell."

"That's a lovely story! This is turning out to be a day of

life stories. Have you found anything else of significance in here?"

"Not yet. I want to go through some more boxes. I am enjoying the memories they unlock and I will keep my eyes open for anything that might be useful for the book."

Chapter Eighteen

It was full dark by the time Ashley and Edmund reached the cottage. She had been right to guess he had not had a chance to eat since breakfast so they set out the picnic as soon as Edmund had managed to wiggle the large iron key enough to open the lock.

The interior was in darkness until Ashley lit the candles setting them into saucers from the tiny kitchen at the back of the cottage.

"Watch your ankles, Ashley! It's pitch black outside the candle's range."

She could not hear this warning very clearly as Edmund had already poured soup into the cup at the top of the flask and was chewing on a bread roll as he spoke.

Once the candles were arrayed around the living room and the torch was standing by for further explorations, they surveyed the accommodations.

"It's definitely cozy, Edmund!" was her summation.

"I don't mind it at all. My mother and father started out in a small row of houses just like this one. It feels like home to me. I can light a fire in the winter evenings and be perfectly comfortable. If I'm right, there will be one bedroom and a small bathroom at the top of the stairs. I can see already, it is a vast improvement on my current lodgings. I don't need much in the way of storage space so this is perfect for me until I see where my next job opportunity leads me."

"So, you don't intend to stay on in Oban, permanently?" For some reason, this thought brought a pang of discomfort to his listener.

"It's not really up to me. I am still gaining experience to decide on my specialization as well as my location. I could go to Edinburgh or Glasgow and work in a big hospital."

"Is that what you would like?" She tried to keep the disappointment out of her voice. She had no right to be concerned in his professional choices. She was not going to be around much longer but it seemed as if Edmund Jansen was a good fit for the small town, at least as far as she had seen, based on his care of her aunt.

"I'm not sure. General Practice has its appeal. Not as exciting as a big hospital with lots of colleagues and drama every day, and yet, there's something about getting to know entire families and building a picture of them over generations that has its own satisfactions. These days, doctors are not as isolated as they once were. It's possible to consult with experts all over the world by internet."

"What would you do if Connor Williams decides to retire?"

"Ah, that could change the picture for me. I'm not sure I am ready to take on a whole practice. Time will tell."

It was the longest conversation they had shared so far. It might be because of the intimate atmosphere created by candlelight and good food, much needed, but Edmund soon sank back into the comfortable small sofa with a sigh of content, bringing his arm into close contact with Ashley's. His head slipped down onto her shoulder and before she knew it he had fallen asleep.

She smiled to herself. *Poor thing, he was exhausted.*

She could not move without waking him, so she sat there

listening to him breathe and watching the candles burn down until they were in darkness once again.

When he finally awoke, disoriented and still sleepy, perhaps still dreaming, he turned to Ashley and kissed her on the mouth.

It took several moments before either of them grasped what had just happened. It was as if something very natural had occurred.

Edmund recovered first. "Oh, God! I am so sorry! I was …….I was dreaming about you."

Ashley, who had been enjoying the closeness of a strong male figure practically lying in her arms for some time, merely responded with, "Don't be sorry, Edmund. I liked it."

She kissed him back with some enthusiasm and he put his arms around her and looked into her eyes to be sure of her consent.

"Don't say anything," she warned him. "Just enjoy the moment."

He did not require any further encouragement and they kissed more deeply, pressed together, content in each other's arms.

When they finally drew apart, Ashley was glad of the dim light from a street lamp. She thought she must look disheveled and somewhat flustered.

Edmund glanced at his watch and drew in his breath when he saw the time.

"It's past midnight. Your aunt will have sent out the police by now."

"I doubt it! She's probably fast asleep. I have my own key. I can slip in quietly and not disturb her."

"Are you……………..are *we* okay?"

"Absolutely! I like your prescription for evening relaxation, but we'd better get on the road. We can talk more tomorrow."

The next day was one of those when everything happens at once. Ashley had scarcely wiped the sleep from her eyes before her aunt was tapping on her bedroom door.

"Are you awake, Ashley?"

"Hmmm, I guess so."

"Good!" The door opened to reveal Anna Drake, fully dressed and pulling on a pair of gloves.

"I'm off for the day with Jeanette and Bev. It turns out Bev is a real fan of the television series 'Outlander' which is based on the novels of Diana Gabaldon. The local newspaper had an article on locations where the new second-season episodes are being shot and one of them is nearby. It will be wonderful to see those familiar faces in realistic eighteenth century costumes acting out the author's exciting adventures."

Though scarcely awake, Ashley could tell how anxious her aunt was to be off.

"I hope it's all right with you, Ashley, and you don't mind being left behind here. We plan to stop in on Fiona on our way home and tell her about our day. Jeanette has a movie camera so you will get to see some of the scenes, if the producers allow it."

"Oh, don't worry about me. I have plenty to do. Off you go on a girls' day out with your best friends. It will do you good. Call me later."

Ashley fell back into the warm nest of her bedclothes and was glad of a promised quiet day to think about last night with Edmund. Anna was not out of the door yet. Her voice drifted up the stairs.

"Oh, I forgot to mention! Last night while you were out, the vet called to say it was possible Sylvia might be delivered today sometime. He's anxious to see how she does on a trial basis. If he arrives, just give me a call. Bye, now!"

Shortly thereafter, the front door shut with a bang and Ashley heard the sound of female laughter as a car revved up and sped down the track.

She glanced at the clock on the mantle over the fireplace

and saw it was still early in the day. A huge yawn escaped her as she calculated how little sleep she had actually had. It had been the early hours of the morning when Edmund eventually dropped her off at the estate house. This thought reminded her of his promise to talk with her today and she wondered how he would get the time since he must also be somewhat the worse for wear after a very busy day with patients. The next thought impelled her to get out of bed and look out of the dormer window to see the weather conditions.

Slipping her feet into sheepskin-lined slippers and pulling the duvet off the bed onto her shivering shoulders, she tiptoed across the room and looked out.

No snow. Sunshine. Blue sky. A beautiful day for her aunt's adventure.

It didn't seem right to crawl back into bed on such a day. She had the house to herself. She had writing and thinking to do and the all-important text to her Canadian Publisher had to be sent. If the illustrated version of Anna's story was to be a reality, Ashley suspected a co-author would be required to handle the technical and artistic parts of the process. She was not sure she was willing to give up her autonomy over the book. It had developed into a very personal project; one for which she felt responsible to her aunt. Had there not been the level of trust between them that had led to her confessions, the book would never have included such intimate moments between Lawren and her aunt. She felt instinctively that these private moments would be the book's primary attraction for readers.

Musing over these points, she threw on some old clothes and went down to the kitchen to seek sustenance for a day of hard work. There, on the table was a breakfast of cereal, bagels with cream cheese and marmalade. The kettle was filled and the brown betty teapot had been warmed with boiled water.

"Exactly what I need," she exclaimed, and set to it with a

vengeance. She was on her second mug of tea when she noticed a hand-written note lying on the table.

Have a good day, Ashley.
I will bring groceries home, so eat whatever you want.
I fancy some bridies for supper and if Sylvia arrives,
I will invite Bev to join us.
Love,
Anna.

Ah, so Callum Moir, may be coming. Edmund might call and I have to contact my publisher, I had better get started before the day is taken up with all kinds of interruptions.

The first interruption was a rather pleasant one. She was working with the office door open and she heard the crunch of a van's wheels. By the time she reached the door and opened it, the young delivery man was holding out a bouquet of flowers for her.

"Miss Stanton? These are for you."

He was gone before she could express her thanks. The card said a simple 'Thank-you' and was signed by Edmund. She blushed, remembering their kisses in the dark and hid her face in the blossoms inhaling the fresh scent. Flowers in the winter were an enormous extravagance and these were pink summer roses, fragrant carnations, white daisies and something exotic she could not name, all enveloped in a variety of greenery. She laid the bouquet on the table while she rummaged around for a suitable vase to contain such bounty.

All thoughts of work flew out of her head. Her first impulse was to call Edmund, but then she thought it could be embarrassing if she enthused over the phone and was overheard by his receptionist or, even worse, by a patient. She decided to wait until later although it was hard to delay when she felt so delighted by his kind gesture.

Leaving the floral display standing on the centre of the kitchen table, where it added a definite festive look to the house, she wandered back to the office and sent off the text to her publisher. She could not summon the energy to begin on the structure of the book again but had an idea of trying to create a title. Somewhere she had read that the title not only catches the attention of the reader, but it can also frame the entire purpose, if chosen with care.

Well, I should do something useful. Perhaps this will help.

She took out a sheet of paper and began to write whatever came into her head.

Anna and Lawren: a Love Story
Lawren Drake; the Man Behind the Portrait
Anna Drake Speaks About her Marriage
Painting a Legacy; A man and His Life.
A Private Couple Revealed: Lawren and Anna Drake.
Oban, Iona and Lawren Drake.

It rapidly became clear, this was not going to be easy. She could see some useful words but none of them immediately declared the perfect title to her, and a perfect title was what she needed.

Could it be the answer to involve Anna in the final decision, thereby taking it out of the author's hands? She was scribbling a pros and cons list about this when the doorbell rang and she jumped out of her seat in surprise.

What now?

The tall, slender figure of Edmund Jansen stood revealed on the doorstep as soon as the red door opened.

"Did the flowers arrive? I asked for immediate delivery. I have only about thirty minutes left in my lunch hour. The staff are covering for me. I just had to see you Ashley. I have been so worried about last night."

"For goodness sake, come inside, Edmund. Come and see your gorgeous flowers for yourself. I love them. It is a lovely gesture but what are you worrying about, and why didn't you warn me you were coming? I look such a mess!"

In answer, he gave her a look that would have melted an iceberg and folded her into his arms for a kiss that made the previous evening's explorations superfluous.

When she could draw breath again, Ashley looked up at him with new eyes. Who was this Lothario who had appeared on the doorstep? Gone were his tentative approaches. This kiss had been felt clear down to her toes and he did not seem to be distracted by her careless clothing. Perhaps he was anxious to make his feelings known in the short time at his disposal this day. Whatever the reason, Ashley Stanton got the message.

"Edmund, sit down for a minute. We need to talk. I think the tea is still hot."

She busied herself with pouring tea while her mind was racing. Declarations of undying devotion were impossible in the present situation but neither did she want to discourage him as a suitor. Genuine feelings were, in her experience, too rare to be disparaged so lightly.

The future was uncertain for both of them. The best she could offer was a pleasant dalliance, as they used to say. How far he chose to take this was an unknown, and yet, her heart was lifted by his interest and his kisses and his presence here. Work had been her focus for years now. She had not had a relationship for longer than she cared to count. Edmund was likely to be in the same situation.

She was saved from the predicament of how to convey this to Edmund, by his next statement.

"Look, Ashley! I know this is sudden, and largely unexpected, but I have to tell you how I feel. Put aside all the impediments for a minute. I don't deny there are plenty in our path. Neither of us is a teenager and we know how disruptive strong emotions can be. I think we are both able to understand how powerful our feelings are. I do want to see you again. Can we say we are dating?"

It was an old-fashioned term, and yet, it seemed appropriate. He had put into words the exact things she had been thinking. She threw caution to the winds and plopped down unceremoniously on his knee, throwing her arms around his neck and pulling him close.

"It is what it is, Edmund. Let's enjoy it!"

He left, ten intense minutes later, with the promise to call and set up their next 'date'. He was hoping Fiona Campbell would allow him to move into the cottage immediately so they could meet there without the town's gossip mill going into high gear. If Fiona agreed, he would speedily get the electricity connected and contact the water company.

Ashley's head was in a spin. She found herself thinking of the cottage as a place she would be spending more time and her aunt's words about the doctor's comforts came back to her. A small electric fire would help as Edmund could hardly be expected to set a wood and coal fire every evening after his work ended. Obviously, an open fire was a fire hazard if he were to be summoned unexpectedly to an emergency house call.

Mixed in with these thoughts was the obligation to move ahead with her writing project. Nothing could be allowed to impede its progress. Anna had made her return to Canada known and the timeline was short. All in all the prospects for a continuing affair with the local doctor were not promising. Each of them had commitments that demanded time and energy.

She sighed and brought her reeling brain under control. This was no whirlwind romance. She did not know how to describe what it actually was.

The scent of his flowers surrounded her and reminded her there was no time to waste from now on if Edmund Jansen was to be a part of her life. She ran upstairs with a song in her heart, to wash and dress in decent clothes then she would work all day on the book, getting her notes into shape and beginning the first chapter. Once that step had been taken, there was no going back. She realized she had been delaying this step for whatever reasons. Dr. Jansen had forced her to forge ahead with her project.

He had already had a good influence on her.

Chapter Nineteen

Ashley was immersed in the world she created when she was writing. Hours sped by. It was not until she felt a pang of hunger that she realized she had not eaten lunch. She decided to bring a coffee into the office so she would not break her productive writing streak. While the water boiled, she was making notes on the back of Anna's letter when she saw a shadow pass across the bay window and looking up she saw an older man carrying an animal cage.

It must be the vet with Sylvia. Damn! Damn ! Damn!

There was nothing else for it. She had to invite him in and pretend to be happy she was being interrupted yet again.

Callum Moir introduced himself quite politely and set the cage on top of the table which she did not think was appropriate. Without asking, he had moved the flower vase to the other end of the table.

He could see she was making coffee so she offered him a cup then asked if he had informed her aunt of his arrival.

"I spoke to Anna on the phone last evening and mentioned my intention to stop by today unless something occurred to prevent me." His tone was now decidedly cool.

Ashley thought it matched her own so she could not complain.

"The reason I ask," she insisted, "is because my aunt told me to tell her if you did arrive. Do you want to talk to her or shall I? She is out with friends for the day."

He quickly deduced that it was preferable if he spoke in person to Anna Drake and so he walked into the larder for privacy leaving Ashley alone with the strange creature.

She had never been a cat lover. In fact she thought most animal owners were somewhat unbalanced in their adoration of small furry pets. She had always been of the mind that the money spent on pets would be better spent on orphaned children or the homeless. But now she had to adjust to the idea of living with this unusual animal for a time.

She sat down with her coffee cup and stared into the cage. It was at her eye level and immediately the gold eyes of a feral creature stared back. This was no timid kitty. Its ears were rather small but its eyes were huge. Its body was long and muscled and its tale was almost the length of its body with thick fur that was bristling up like a brush, at her gaze.

Other than the eyes, she thought the only remarkable feature was the colour of its fur; a brindled combination of brown, black and gold, almost in stripes but broken up for camouflage purposes, she presumed.

So this was Sylvia, the female version of the male wildcat Sylvester who had lived in this kitchen with Anna and Fiona for some weeks.

Personally, Ashley could not see the attraction. Sylvia was rather ugly, in fact. The possibility that the feeling was mutual did not occur to her.

She could hear the rise and fall of voices from the larder. Callum Moir emerged with a disgruntled look on his face. He was not pleased to have missed seeing Anna and he was reluctant to take the cage away again.

"Would you be capable of watching over Sylvia until your aunt arrives home?"

"Just a minute! I know nothing about this animal and I don't want to be held responsible for its safety."

"Ach, there's no danger to you, lassie. She'll be fine in the cage for now. I'll put a dish of water and some food inside for her. I saw supplies in the larder there. She can wait under the counter and she'll likely sleep until later when Anna can settle her in her new home."

Ashley had to be content with this arrangement. She was determined to take no part in the cat's care. As soon as she could get the vet out of the house she was going back to work.

※

Anna Drake felt like a child given an unexpected day off school. Just spending time with her friends would have been reward enough, but to be off on an unexpected adventure in Scotland was beyond anything she could have hoped for. Her spirits rose with every mile and the atmosphere in the car was light-hearted and a trifle raucous.

"You did not say that!" accused Bev, when Jeanette regaled them with her account of a recent customer's refusal to pay his bill.

"I damn well did!" she declared. "He gave me a ton of grief over his stupid wallpaper and there was no way he was going to guilt me into paying for his mistakes."

"But what did his wife say?" Anna was having trouble speaking through her laughter.

"Oh she was a little mouse, unfortunately. She never dared to express her opinion. As far as I am concerned, she deserves the ghastly wine and black mess on her dining room wall. They'll be looking at it for years to come. The stuff was so heavily embossed and so deeply coloured that there's no chance of painting over it, and the glue required to make it adhere to the wall was like cement. It's there till the house falls down, I tell you."

The car seemed to shake with the gales of laughter these comments created. Anna could not remember the last time she had laughed so hard or so easily. She felt a cloud lift from her mind; a cloud that had darkened her thoughts for a long period, perhaps as long as since Lawren had died. It might be related to the lightness she experienced once she had revealed to Ashley the details of his death, or it might be the effect of the scenery she could see from the car. Whichever, she was enjoying the feeling.

It was a beautiful gift of a day coming after the first real warnings of approaching winter. The earth had reneged on its promise and restored one glorious, late Fall reminder of the season that was passing. The sky was a clear blue, the fields had cast off the remnants of snow and returned to their final green glory interspersed with banks of purple heather climbing up the lower slopes of the mountains in the distance. The trees were about to shake off their lingering leaves as soon as the next chill winds blew in, but for now all was perfect and peaceful around them.

"It's so good to hear you so sounding carefree, Anna." Bev had taken her friend's arm and whispered in her ear.

Jeanette was swearing in unladylike fashion at the GPS which was supposed to be taking them to some obscure destination where the day's shooting was scheduled.

"It says I'm to turn here and drive for three miles along this winding trail that looks to be heading upward. I doubt the film crew could get their big trailers up here but George assured me the GPS thing works so we'd better give it a try. Hang on you two!"

Jeanette's warning came just in time as the trail was rough and littered with stones washed down from the hills in the recent rains. Bumping up and down made the women slightly hysterical but they were game for anything as long as they were together.

After what seemed like five miles, two huge trucks appeared on the horizon beside the ruins of an old castle or fortress. All three women shouted with glee and were soon approached by a uniformed guard who cautioned them to be quiet and park to the side in a field with several other cars.

"You ladies must be verra respectful and you canna bother the actors. The director has not much patience the day. He was planning on dull and grey weather for atmosphere and this braw sunshine is not tae his liking, ye ken?"

They hushed each other until more demure attitudes were achieved, and then they crept across the field in the wake of the guard until they could see an amazing sight suddenly emerge within the walls of a grimy courtyard. They huddled together on benches placed on top of a stone platform with a handful of other excited spectators. So much was happening that it was difficult at first to focus. Bev nudged Anna and pointed to the horses standing with their handlers. Jeanette was watching the set being speedily erected in a corner so that it was transformed into a stall with vegetables and loaves of bread for sale. A group of women in long, trailing, woollen skirts were standing in a huddle to one side smoking cigarettes and waiting for instructions. Across the floor of the set ran a metal track along which the camera could speed while following the action.

Anna checked out all the actors but could see no one who looked like dark-haired Claire or red-headed Jamie. She wondered if the stars would appear at all. This could be a minor scene involving only secondary characters, but fascinating all the same, to see the eighteenth century recreated on a modern Scottish hillside. Of course, the hillside and the ruined fort were not much changed in the last centuries.

This thought hit Anna with the power of a revelation. She had a sense of time passing; places and people disappearing from the land; buildings disintegrating, kings and warriors obliterated, but the land endures. All at once she wanted to be alone to think of Lawren in this landscape. He was one of those who had lived and loved and gone, never to return, but always to be remembered.

The director was calling loudly for silence as the actors moved into place. All eyes were on the busy set and Anna slipped away by herself, murmuring something about fetching a scarf from the car.

She spotted a lone tree on the hillside above the parked cars and was drawn toward it. Her heart was heavy with loss as she stood with her back to the tree trunk. It was then she cast her gaze upward and saw a magnificent view. Hills and glens stretching up to the high mountains that spoke to her of timeless endurance.

"I to the hills will lift mine eyes," she whispered, "From whence doth come mine aid."

The old words gave comfort and the pain in her heart gradually faded again.

She knew deep within her, that the one to whom you have given your heart cannot ever be far away.

The wind came rushing down the valley and rattled the leaves on the tree beneath which she stood.

The glorious day was coming to an end. She had left her coat on the wooden bench where Bev and Jeanette waited and now she needed its protection.

She slipped back into her seat and Bev turned to her and said, "Did you see that? The swordplay looked so real but the choreographer stopped the men several times and reset their positions. Who knew so much effort went into one short scene? It's amazing!"

Jeanette replied, "I'll never watch television again without appreciating how many people and their unique skills go into a production. Oh, look! Here come Jamie and Murtagh. Don't they look magnificent on their horses? And those tartan plaids splayed out along the horses' rear quarters are just splendid.

I am so glad we came!"

Anna soon became lost in the scene playing out before her.

They could not hear all the dialogue and often found the main characters obscured by sound boards or lighting screens but it was fascinating to get a peek at how it all came together.

Finally, the director called, "That's a take! Thank you everyone. We'll call it a day before the light fades."

Jeanette jumped up and led the way back to the car. Bev told Anna their friend wanted to get ahead of the other cars or they would be hours getting back to the main road again.

Anna was quiet on the return trip. Her two friends chatted on about what they had seen but Anna was pleasantly tired and content to listen. When they arrived at Fiona's house in the forest, she met them at her front door with the baby in her arms and declared she was coming with them in her own car as Ashley had phoned to say Sylvia had been delivered and she was terrified there might be something wrong with the cat.

"Why? What's happened?" asked Anna in some alarm.

"Ashley couldn't tell me. She said the cat was growling at her all the time and she was afraid it would injure itself trying to get out of the cage."

Some discussion ensued and the conclusion was for Bev and Anna to go with Fiona to the estate house while Jeanette drove home to her family.

Fiona knew about the plan to buy food for a meal at Anna's. She had raided her own larder and placed a basket in the boot of the car. As soon as the baby had been handed to his father, they set out to drive through the town and out onto the country road at a pace that reminded Anna of Fiona's younger days driving a shared taxi with Grant, Cameron's father.

"What on earth could be wrong?" she asked.

"I really don't know. The kitten was in good shape when Callum collected her from our shed. It's always possible she did not respond well to the cage, or to the car, but she had lots of gentle handling from Fergus and Shona so she should be accustomed to humans by now."

They rocketed into the lane leading to the estate house gate and Anna was out of the car as soon as the engine shut off. As she ran up the path she could hear the loud yowling sounds of an animal in distress.

Ashley met them at the door.

"I'm so sorry! I couldn't reach your phone so I called Fiona. I couldn't get a lick of work done with the awful noise the cat is making. I've never heard such a sound coming from such a small creature. What did I do wrong?"

Anna patted her arm reassuringly, and with Fiona right behind her, she walked quietly into the kitchen and soon found the cage under the bottom shelf in the larder.

Sylvia was still frantically trying to climb out of the metal cage with no success. She had upturned the water dish and the food dish and had wet kibble stuck to her paws. Fiona began to speak to the kitten in soft tones which had the effect of stopping the howling, while Anna undid the latch holding the front section of the cage. Immediately, the cat moved forward warily and sniffed the two women, then she ventured out of the despised cage and rushed under the kitchen table. Anna made sure the door to the entry hall was shut. It was going to be necessary to keep the cat secured in one area until she felt safe again. Fiona was still coaxing Sylvia to be calm with her quiet voice and gentle soothing sounds and Anna remembered their days with Sylvester in the cupboard while they worked together to save his life.

Sylvia was much bigger than the poor helpless wildcat had been. She seemed much happier now she had been freed from her prison. Her next move was over to the window seat where she sniffed the cushion eagerly and finally curled up with her nose on her paws, with her long tail curling over both and settled to sleep.

Fiona and Anna smiled. Sylvia had chosen Morag's favourite spot. Bev, who had been waiting to see what would happen, also recalled fond memories of the brown tabby who had lived in both farmhouses.

Ashley, noticing the sudden silence from the other side of the kitchen door, dared to open it an inch to see if everyone was still alive.

"It's all right now, Ashley. Come in. She's asleep, poor wee thing. She must be exhausted. The vet should have known better than to leave her here without any comforts."

Fiona had taken a seat on the window bench, still making soothing sounds and stroking the kitten's fur.

"Ashley, please go and fetch the basket from the car. There's salad and quiche and fruit in there. We can eat in the lounge and give her some peace till she settles down."

Ashley sped down the path, glad to get away from the chaos of the cat's arrival. She would have been quite happy to eat in the car but that would be revealing her distaste for the animal and considering how delighted the three older women were about the noisy invader, she would not be endearing herself to them by doing so.

She found the basket, heavy with food supplies, and took it back inside the house, spreading the feast out on the office desk so everyone could help themselves and sit on the couch, or the chairs by the lounge fireside, in comfort. She put a match to the fire. The fine day had cooled and any room outside of the kitchen was going to be cold this evening.

Anna soon appeared with dishes and silverware. Fiona was filling the teapot with boiling water from the kettle on top of the Aga and she soon arrived with glasses and a bottle of wine as well as tea cups.

Since the office door was open, the conversation soon turned to the subject of the book Ashley was writing.

"How far along are you? What have you discovered? Who have you talked to?"

The real question Bev and Fiona wanted to ask was, 'How does Anna feel about this?' but neither wished to embarrass their hostess or her great-niece.

Sensing the unspoken question, however, Anna decided it was time to make clear her total support for the book.

"Ashley has been very patient with me. She is a good listener and I have been able to open up to her here in the house in a way I have not been comfortable with before. She is in charge of what will be included in the book but I am sure I will have final say over anything too personal."

From her seat by the fireside, Bev commented, "It sounds as if you have unburdened yourself of some troublesome memories, Anna. Am I right?"

"Yes. Something about my illness and being confined to bed made me appreciate my responsibility to share more about my years with Lawren and to let the art world know him as a man as well as a consummate artist. It feels right to do it now. After all none of us has forever."

Everyone in the room knew Anna was thinking of Lawren's sudden death. Only two of them knew the remarkable details, however, and Ashley was determined to change that.

Fiona got up and put down her cup. "I have to be getting home to my wee bairn. Gordon is very good with him but he can't substitute for a mother's breast."

The women nodded and smiled. Fiona went over to Anna, looked her in the face then pulled her into a huge hug, whispering in her ear as she did so. Ashley, who was nearest, heard the word 'godmother'.

It was a signal for the day to end. Fiona took away the empty dishes and reminded Anna to call her with an update on Sylvia's progress. Bev said she would be back in the morning and she left with Fiona for the short ride home. Anna tiptoed into the kitchen and brought back the despised cage, now cleaned out, setting it on the window seat beside the cat with a soft pillow bed inside and a litter tray and water bowl.

As the house emptied, there was one last interruption for

Ashley. Her phone in the office chimed and she rushed to answer it before the cat's yowling could start up again.

"Ashley Stanton? This is Warren Brady. I hope it's not too late to bother you?"

"No! No, Warren. I am delighted you returned my call so quickly. What did you think about the illustrated book idea?"

"Well, my girl, you certainly set the cat among the pigeons over here. Our phones have been ringing all day with calls from Ottawa, New York and London, of course. That's both Londons, by the way!"

"But what's going on?"

"You must have known new works by Lawren Drake would get a lot of attention. The single photo you sent was quite enough to start a buying frenzy. A self-portrait? It's a rarity these days."

"But, what about the book? Are illustrations going to push up the price and interest more buyers?"

"That might work, Ash. The reaction seems to indicate a separate publication for the art lovers with high photographic quality. More of a coffee table book; you know the kind of thing."

Ashley knew exactly what he meant and it was far from the reader-friendly biography she had envisioned for Anna's story. She saw the book idea fading into the background and with it went her input.

"Listen, Warren! I don't want to play hardball here, but you must realize the drawings and the text are at my great-aunt's discretion and she has entrusted both to me. I need to know you support the book first and foremost. I can assure you it will be just as stunning in its own way as the drawings. Oh, in case you are in any doubt, I am reserving a copy of one of Lawren Drake's drawings for the cover of *my book*."

She paused to catch her breath. She had placed a deal of emphasis on the last two words and she was aware she might have gone a little too far with an important Canadian publisher.

There was a brief pause on the line. Ashley gritted her teeth.

"Right! I see what you are saying. Let me get back to you tomorrow. You seem to hold all the cards for now, young Ashley. So, with the vital Christmas market in mind, how fast can you get the book ready for print? Give me the title and send a chapter for approval and we'll see what we can do."

Ashley exhaled. There was still a chance the book would go ahead but it was imperative Warren Brady thought she was prepared to send her book draft for approval as soon as possible. She shuffled the paper on her desk until she uncovered the list of titles and chose the first one that appealed to her.

"I have a title. It's this, A Private Couple Revealed: Anna and Lawren Drake."

"Hmmm….. the personal approach. I like it! If your text matches in quality and purpose, we could make both ideas work. Oh, I may have to send a British expert to you to assess the market value of the drawings. I'll be in touch about that."

"I'll send a word document to you tomorrow, Warren. Thanks again."

She clicked off before he could demand more evidence. She was five hours ahead of North American time which gave her all night and most of the morning to knock the first chapter into shape and write it in such a way as to convince Warren Brady of the financial viability of Anna's story.

With her head spinning, she opened her laptop and began to make crucial decisions for chapter one.

- Start with Anna meeting Lawren on her London condo doorstep?
- Skip ahead to the first visit to his studio and the impressions she gained there?
- Introduce Susan and the boardroom portraits?
- Describe the Three Women painting that she had exclusive access to, as a beginning point?

- Start with Anna's description of Lawren's death and work in a flashback from there?

Anna looked into the lounge and saw Ashley with her laptop open, typing away at a furious rate.

She hesitated to interrupt to ask about the phone call and decided to wait until morning. It had been an unusual day and she was tired. She would light the fire in her own bedroom for comfort and add peat to the lounge fire so Ashley would stay warm. She noticed the tartan shawl on the back of the desk chair.

Sylvia was fast asleep.

Ashley was fine. Anna could rest undisturbed.

Chapter Twenty

Edmund Jansen survived his long days at the surgery by visualizing how sweet it would be to go to his little cottage at the end of the day. He imagined the scene would include the lovely Ashley and there would be cozy sessions by the fireside with the sound of waves crashing on the shoreline outside and wind whistling in the chimneypots above.

The weather seemed to cooperate with his plan but that was all. Cold winds blew a storm in from the Atlantic every two or three days. Clouds obscured the sky and an endless line of coughing, sneezing, bronchial patients assembled in the waiting room. He began to count the hours until old Doctor Williams was due to return.

Ashley was not responding to his calls and that was worrying. Had he said or done something to upset her the last time they were together? He called the farmhouse line and Anna reported Ashley was well but had some kind of work deadline to meet.

The one positive note in the week was that Fiona Campbell agreed to his request to start renting the cottage immediately and she took on the task of contacting the services to make sure everything was in order for his occupancy. He would have been happy to forego water and electricity if only he could vacate his present miserable apartment over the store on the High Street. As soon as he had known there was an alternative, what had previously been less than attractive living conditions, suddenly became unbearable and he packed what little he possessed ready to move out at a moment's notice. The envelope with his last month's rent was already waiting for the landlord.

In the meantime, he contacted his mother and brought her up to date with recent developments.

"Ed, this is good news about the cottage. It will give me a better idea of your surroundings since I can imagine exactly what it is like. How are you feeling regards staying in Oban? Don't you want to work closer to home now?"

"Mum, I am nowhere near making a final decision. There's a lot to think about. I'll talk to you more when I come home for Christmas. I do like it here, however. I've made some friends and you know how difficult it is to do that when I have the doctor label on me. Nearly everyone I meet is either a patient or someone who wants free medical advice."

"Well, I must say you sound more cheerful than the last time you called. What's changed things?"

His mother was far too intuitive about him. She always had a sixth sense about what he was feeling.

He thought of trying to distract her by referring again to the cottage, but he had a sudden notion of inviting Ashley to meet his mother over Christmas and if that were to happen, it would be better to prepare the ground now.

"I will say I have met a lovely young woman here. She's related to one of my patients. Her name is Ashley Stanton, but please don't pester me for more details. It's very early days yet and I don't want to jinx the whole thing by giving you unrealistic expectations. She lives in Canada, by the way."

Christine Jansen had to damp down her excitement but some of it leaked across the phone line in spite of her best efforts. For some years she had thought her Edmund would never find a girlfriend and she would never be a grandmother.

"That *is* good news Ed. I look forward to meeting her someday but I will wait for an invitation of course. Don't you worry about that. Call me again when you get settled into the cottage and do try to get some sleep. You know you work too hard, just like your father did."

So, she played the 'father' card although she knows I can't say anything more now. I may have set off a firestorm of curiosity but it felt like the right thing to do. Right; but not safe. I am jumping the gun here and I must remain cool if I want to build on Ashley's interest. I really need time to figure out my next move. Turning up uninvited could be a mistake, especially if she is busy. I wonder what kind of work she is involved in? Obviously something she can do from home.

A knock at the office door signaled the end of his lunch break. As soon as he exited he could hear the cacophony of noises in the waiting room. Everything from strenuous nose blowing to deep hacking coughing could be heard. It was going to be another very busy afternoon at the surgery.

Christine Jansen put down her phone and sat down immediately to take full measure of the news her son had conveyed. This Ashley person was a surprise and yet, if she lived in Canada, was there much hope of a steady relationship? She chided herself for old-fashioned ideas. These days, couples lived and worked all over the globe and many seemed to be able to make a marriage, or other serious partnership, work for them.

She was also concerned about Edmund's situation in the medical field. This was an old worry and she sighed in frustration as she thought of it. She had tried to discourage her son from following in the footsteps of his father; a path that had led to his early death from what she insisted was overwork and not any real ailment. A part of her heart was always in fear her Edmund might succumb to the same dire fate.

But what could a mother do? He was a talented, hard-working man who wanted to make a difference in the world by applying his many skills. She could not stand in his way, despite her fears. He was his father's son all right. The way it seemed now, both her men, in different ways, had left her too soon.

A hot tear slid down her cheek. She sent up a silent prayer. Whoever Ashley Stanton was, a mother's hopes lay in her hands.

※

As the days went by, Ashley was aware of, and grateful for, her aunt's absorption in the care and feeding of Sylvia. Bev was a second nursemaid for the cat and Ashley could hear them discussing food, water, bedding, and when they would be able to let the creature roam further than the kitchen.

There had been one angry call to the vet, and his excuses accepted, but he kept away, which pleased Ashley greatly.

She was deep into the book's structure now and was keeping her publisher at bay by forwarding a chapter a day to his editor. She had no time for interruptions of any kind and barely finished the food left for her in the lounge. It took every ounce of her strength and concentration to forge a chapter each day and ensure it was worthy of the ones that had already been sent.

To her great relief, Warren Brady had not pointed out anything objectionable thus far. He was content to let her speed ahead as fast as possible with an eye to the lucrative Christmas book sales market and had already begun the process of designing a suitable cover, using the title and sketch she had suggested. He remained positive about the possibility of producing the memoir before the Christmas deadlines and remarked how fortunate it was that digital printing technology allowed him to make electronic copies of Ashley's chapters as soon as they were received and edited.

Naturally, Ashley did not indicate how frantically she was working to keep up with the punishing schedule. The writing was progressing well, so far, but if she faltered it would have serious consequences.

She allowed Anna to field all phone calls and take messages. She could not dare to break her concentration for any reason. It was at the end of her long day when she finally took time to read the messages. Four were from Edmund and she put these aside with a sigh. He would have to wait.

One was from Warren giving her the name and authority of an art dealer from Edinburgh who was to arrive in Oban within three days. She was instructed to gather the new Drake sketches for a Gregor Mackintosh's perusal. This task she immediately passed on to her aunt then dragged herself up to bed before she could be inveigled into any conversation about her progress. Only by getting a few hours of restful sleep could she continue at this frantic pace and the thought that she might break down or lose focus was a constant fear.

As instructed, Anna Drake returned to the cedar closet the following day to look for more evidence of Lawren's sketches. This was a pleasant task; something of a treasure hunt. She had opened all the boxes without finding more of Lawren's work than Ashley had originally uncovered. She did find an unexpected legacy of her beneficiary, Helen Dunlop. In a small ivory container she found a selection of very beautiful antique hair clasps. Anna vaguely remembered seeing these years before, but as her own hair had been cut in a short style for a long time she had put the collection aside. Now the box had turned up between two books on the shelves she had begun to look through. Many of the books had belonged to Helen Dunlop and were initially in the garage in large storage boxes but Anna hoped to find something else of Lawren's that had been put away for safekeeping when the estate house was rented.

She piled up several gardening reference books for Fiona's new garden including one large tome with full-page illustrations of the kind of perfect plants only seen in such publications, when some pages fell out. Tut tutting to herself about such carelessness with a book, she picked them up to deposit on top of the pile and stopped as she caught sight of the pencil drawings. At first these did not look anything like the full-size sketches Ashley had uncovered. The pages were smaller and the drawings were crowded onto the paper in haphazard order. It took a moment to recognize Lawren's style on a much smaller scale and then another moment to understand that she was the subject. It looked like he had been watching her from their bedroom window while she planted herbs, or hung out washing, or fetched fuel from the shed in the rear garden. These were everyday activities and would be of no interest except that he had managed to imbue the simple outlines with the magic of his emotions.

Anna felt a sob rise up from her chest at the realization of how much Lawren had loved her. It was clear in every line and every mark of the pencil. She had been given a gift by finding these now. It felt as if Lawren was approving of the plan to reveal more of their life to the world in Ashley's book.

Immediately after she had concluded this, she knew what to do. She ran downstairs to the office with the pages in her hand and called out to Ashley to warn her to stop typing.

"Look, Ashley! Look what I've just found!"

Ashley turned with a frown on her face at this alarming noise. She was transcribing from her recorder and hated to stop in mid-sentence, but her Aunt Anna was definitely excited about something. Hopefully, it was not the cat escaping to rampage around the house!

Anna thrust the pages onto Ashley's knees. "These were hidden inside a book. They are quite domestic and could be the ones you need to illustrate your book. What do you think?"

She turned the pages over and saw they were all about Anna in the house and garden in Oban.

She knew immediately these were perfect for the book. They lacked the finished detail of the larger drawings but their scale was exactly what the personal story needed. She debated whether or not she should keep them from the art expert and decided he was not likely to want them when he saw the larger, more significant, finished sketches. She would be happy to add these to the text she was currently writing. They gave insight into the daily tasks Lawren had shared with Anna in their Scottish hideaway and, as they had never been seen before, they were an added incentive for art lovers to purchase the book.

As if on cue, the phone rang in the kitchen and Anna ran off to intercept the call, returning a minute later with the news that a Gregor Mackintosh would be arriving within the hour to peruse certain sketches.

"Oh, darn! What does he sound like?"

"Well, rather a 'stuffed shirt,' as they say; a very British Public School type, from his voice. He said he was in a hurry and needs to see everything at once."

"Oh, dear! I had better prepare the exhibits and take the chance to grab something to eat then I must get back to work. I can't afford to fall behind."

Gregor Mackintosh arrived on the dot of three o'clock, precisely one minute less than the hour he had predicted on the phone. Ashley and Anna awaited him in the kitchen with the sketches arrayed across the kitchen table and Sylvia confined to her cage in the larder out of sight.

Ashley had managed to eat a sandwich and gulp a cup of tea after taking scant time to change her clothes and tidy her hair, pinning the length back with one of the lovely clasps her

Aunt Anna brought to her. She chose a heavy, gold-coloured, oval-shaped one with a crimson stone under a tracery of gold metal patterns in the hopes it might make up for the lack of adornment in her other clothing. She had not taken time to bathe or shower in the last few days and had grabbed the first clean item she found in her bedroom wardrobe.

As soon as she beheld the splendour of Gregor Mackintosh, Ashley felt unkempt, unprepared and uncouth. The Highland gentleman, for that was who he gave every evidence of being, could not have been more formally dressed. He wore the kilt of his clan with sporran and knee socks and even a skean dhu tucked into the folded-over cuff. His double-breasted black velvet jacket with resplendent silver buttons concealed a white, starched, dress shirt. All of this was revealed when he removed his long dark overcoat.

Anna's eyebrows were at full alert and Ashley was struck dumb until he began by apologizing for his appearance.

"I received an urgent call from an overseas contact and as I am on my way to a wedding in Fort William, I thought to combine the two events in one trip. I hope you ladies do not mind."

He had one of those mesmerizing, soft Scottish accents that imbues even the simplest words with an intimacy and sincerity that cannot be denied. Anna emerged from the fog of amazement first, and assured him she was not in any way objecting to his outfit. She offered a cup of tea which he accepted, provided he could drink it without any water or other liquid approaching the table. His eye had lighted on the sketches within seconds of being shepherded into the kitchen.

Anna retired to the larder to make the tea while Ashley tried valiantly to compose a sentence to indicate she was not mute. He was certainly a sight to behold; quite enough to strike any female speechless.

"Tell me about the sketches," he asked, as he patrolled the perimeter of the large table. "Where were they discovered, in what condition, and for how long had they been hidden from view?"

Ashley scrambled to answer these questions to the best of her ability. She must have satisfied his curiosity because he nodded happily when he discovered the location had been in a cedar closet, not a musty cellar or damp attic. She followed him around the table feeling dwarfed by his height and the width of his velvet-clad shoulders but watching the delicacy of his long fingers as he carefully lifted and examined each sketch in turn.

Gregor Mackintosh refrained from issuing an opinion until he had stepped back from the table and finished his tea. He was about to speak when his attention was diverted by a strange sound.

"Good Lord! What is that? Is there a wild animal somewhere in your kitchen Mrs. Drake?"

Anna and her niece exchanged glances but there was no way to conceal the truth. Anna embarked on the tale of Sylvia and they saw his amazement grow with every word.

"You mean an actual wildcat kit is living here with you?"

"Well to be accurate, it is a hybrid and immune from the Scottish wildlife laws. We suspect the mother was a large domestic cat and the father a true wildcat."

"Indeed! May I see the creature? It is a rare experience to catch sight of one *anywhere* these days, never mind in a kitchen!"

Anna invited him to follow her into the larder where he promptly went down on his knees to peer inside the cage.

Sylvia reacted with predictable animosity, growling at the stranger's smell and baring a set of remarkable sharp teeth. Gregor Mackintosh was not put off by the display of aggression. He seemed to be familiar with the ways of cats. Anna counted that in his favour.

"Why, she's a beauty all right! Does she get out of the cage at all? I would appreciate a look at her on the move, as it were. Of course, the sketches would have to be safely removed first."

Anna was intrigued enough to attempt a meeting between Sylvia and this stranger but both she and Ashley needed to hear his professional opinion about the sketches before they went any further to please Mr. Mackintosh.

"We could arrange that for you, after you give us your assessment." She gestured toward the kitchen table and he immediately stood up and brushed off his knees, straightening his velvet jacket and standing tall.

"Excuse me, ladies. I was distracted from my purpose here. The provenance of the Drake sketches is not in any doubt whatsoever. Therefore, they are of great value in the art world. I will report to my dealers in England and in Canada that they are authentic, and previously unseen, examples of his work. These will be added to the catalogue that already contains many other remarkable sketches Lawren Drake completed on his journey in Wiltshire some years ago.

In due course, a conservation expert will arrive here to take charge of the sketches and arrange for their transport to Canada for publication. He will bring a photographer to record them for insurance purposes. Here is his card. I hope I don't need to tell you to replace these sketches in the cedar closet and to protect them.

In time, you, Mrs. Drake, as the owner, will be receiving a rather large sum of money."

He stopped short and a look of distress passed over his craggy face.

"Forgive me! I am presuming you do wish to sell them?"

Anna felt a fleeting sense of parting as she thought of losing the sketches but they had been in her possession for such a short time that she had not developed an attachment to them. She looked over at Ashley and considered her role in the publication of the art book as well as the biographical book she was now immersed in. At some point, Anna figured she could get copies of the sketches to keep and in the meantime she would be content with the smaller, less-grand poses she had found upstairs. There was, however, one exception.

"Mr. Mackintosh, would you please note that, as the owner, I must have in my possession a full-size photocopy of Lawren Drake's self-portrait before any of these sketches could leave my hands."

"My dear lady, it is well within your rights to require this. Duly noted. I can promise it will be done."

Anna nodded her approval. "As to your enquiry about selling my husband's sketches.... "

She stopped.

The Edinburgh art expert berated himself silently for not establishing the lady's intentions earlier.

Two pairs of eyes watched Anna Drake's face as she deliberated her answer to Gregor Mackintosh's question. Ashley knew it was her aunt's decision exclusively, but one that would affect her own future career.

"I am an old lady now, Mr. Mackintosh. It is in my best interests to secure my late husband's legacy while I am alive. I believe we can trust your advice and your integrity in this matter."

Ashley bent her head in relief.

Gregor Mackintosh took Anna's hand and bowed over it. "Thank you, dear lady, for your confidence in me. I will not disappoint you in any way. It has been my privilege to meet you in your lovely home."

The atmosphere in the room lightened at once.

Anna asked Ashley to remove the sketches and take them back to safe storage.

Gregor watched while Ashley did this with great care, interleafing the sketches with pages of clean paper from her printer supply.

When her niece had left the kitchen, Anna brought in Sylvia's cage and placed it on the window seat, advising the tall man to stand back in case there was a reaction to his presence. She knew a wildcat was capable of spitting powerfully to discourage unwanted attention.

Sylvia responded by behaving beautifully for the visitor. She stepped out of her confinement with a stately air and stretched first her back legs and then her front, showing the claws to advantage. It was as if she cautioned the stranger not to threaten her owner in any way. Sylvia permitted Anna to smooth down her ruffled fur with one gentle stroke and then turned her back and paraded slowly to her chosen perch with a view out of the window, ignoring the spectator.

Gregor gasped. "She is magnificent! I imagine you are not concerned about the size she is likely to achieve?"

"Not at all! Her predecessor was not permitted to live out his life here but Sylvia will stay in this home.

Thanks to the work of a dear friend of mine, and others, the purebred wildcat is beginning to make a comeback in Scotland."

"Would that friend be Gordon Campbell? I have heard of his work."

"Indeed it is! His wife, Fiona, was my partner in saving the life of Sylvester some years ago. They are a couple dedicated to wildlife preservation on their estate at Glenmorie Castle."

"Ah, indeed! I would be most obliged if you could possibly secure me an introduction to the Campbells. Art is not my only interest."

"I think I can promise that at some future time."

"Wonderful! I will keep in touch. Here is my card with all my contact information. Thank you so much for today. I will have plenty to talk about at my cousin's wedding in Fort William."

He seemed to suddenly remember his destination and glanced at the time. With his overcoat, he donned his professional manner and was about to leave when Ashley returned to the kitchen.

"If I may be so bold, Miss Stanton, I also have an interest

in antique jewellery and, unless I am greatly mistaken, the clasp on your hair is made of gold and garnet by a renowned Scottish craftsman. It looks charming on you, and I am glad to see it in use. However, because of its value, I would handle it with the greatest care."

With that, he exited, leaving in his wake, two women with open mouths and much to discuss.

Chapter Twenty-One

It did not take long for Ashley to realize she had another addition for her book.

Gregor Mackintosh was a writer's gift. Such a colourful character does not come along every day.

His arrival at the estate house was, after all, an integral part of the story of Anna and Lawren.

It was not only his charming manner and earnest compliments that had fascinated his listeners.

His information had given Ashley and Anna something to celebrate. Anna had been told she would benefit from the sales of Lawren's sketches, as used in the proposed art book. Ashley assured her aunt she would also receive royalties from the sales of her biography book, not to mention the value of the antique hair clasps left by Helen Dunlop.

"Well!" announced Anna, as the two women tried to calm down from a bout of ridiculous excitement by imbibing a second and third cup of tea, "I stand by my decision to give you Helen's hair adornments as I can't use them. That is, unless you would rather sell them, Ashley?"

It was something she would have to consider. If the remaining clasps were of equal value to the one Gregor Macintosh saw, selling them would bring in some much-needed cash. Other than those who were lucky enough to write a real blockbuster, most authors earned little from a book by the time the publisher had taken his cut.

"If you are serious about this generous offer, I am thrilled to have them. I can promise you this particular clasp will never be sold. I will, however, wash and style my hair before wearing it again!"

The day's writing schedule had been shattered by the advent of the Scotsman's arrival. Ashley saw, from the kitchen window where Sylvia still slept with her tail over her nose, the glow of sunset staining the clouds.

She knew it was going to be another long night of work.

The chapter was finished, although several hours late. Ashley was about to climb the stairs to bed in the early hours of the morning when the phone shrilled as she was passing the kitchen.

Darn! This will wake my aunt if I don't answer now. She grabbed the phone on the fourth ring.

"Whoever this is, it had better be important at this hour!"

"Oops! Sorry, Ashley, I just got back from a house call out of town and I guess I didn't check the time.

I've been anxious to talk to you for several days now, but you have been difficult to reach. Is there a message in that?"

She took a breath and softened the angry tone of voice he had just heard her use.

"Edmund, I must apologize. I have a deadline to get my book to the publisher and I haven't even left the house for days. I should have told you before, but there has been such a lot going on here and I forgot. As to your question, there isn't a message there, other than the urgency of my project."

"I see. Well, I would love to hear about your book when you can manage the time. I wanted you to know, thanks to Fiona Campbell's efforts, I have moved into the cottage and it is perfect for me, as I suspected. Call me when you can, Ashley. I owe you a meal."

The thought of a meal by the fireside with Edmund had instant appeal. He was one of the life items she had cast aside in favour of the daily chapter. If she could manage to double up one day, she could take the time to re-establish their relationship. A huge yawn interrupted this chain of thought and Ashley crawled into bed just as her aunt was about to greet the day.

Anna Mason Drake was well aware of the pressure her niece was under in order to complete the book on time. When an urgent call came for Ashley from Kate, who introduced herself as the book's editor, Anna knew Ashley was still asleep rather than beavering away all day as was expected. Anna had little sympathy with the publisher's deadlines so she did not feel inclined to honour Kate's request to wake her niece.

"You see, Mrs. Drake, I must know how the next chapter begins. I have an idea to revamp the last three chapters. I discussed it with Ashley and now it's imperative that I hear the first sentence. It will tell me if she is moving in the right direction. So, is Ashley not available?"

"No, she is not. You have been pushing her hard for this material and she is temporarily unable to come to the phone."

"Don't say she's ill!" The horror of this possible calamity came through clearly in Kate's voice and it did nothing to endear her to her listener.

"Before you ask, I will not go and wake her from a well-deserved sleep, Kate. You will just have to wait. If she continues at this pace, illness is not out of the question."

"No, you don't understand, Mrs. Drake, this is essential."

"You did use the word 'imperative'. I think I got the message but it does not change my mind."

There was a pause on the line. Anna had finished what

she wanted to say and was on the verge of putting down the phone when Kate tried again.

"I do apologize! I have been exceedingly rude. Could I request a compromise that won't involve Ashley at all?"

"I can't imagine what that would be." The woman was becoming downright annoying and Anna did not like her persistence.

"Look! If you would be so good as to open Ashley's document and read me the first sentence of her latest chapter, I will be able to get on with my work and she will be able to continue when she is ready."

Anna was incensed. This woman was pushy and inappropriate. Anna was beginning to understand Ashley's obvious feelings of pressure.

"I'm afraid that is out of the question. I could not impose on Ashley's work. What if I accidently erased something important? It's unthinkable!"

Kate recognized an impasse when she heard one. There was no moving Anna Drake. She seemed to be quite a formidable person.

"Can I ask you to tell Ashley to contact me immediately when she is available? I'll give you my direct line in the office and my email."

The change in tone mollified Anna to some degree and she agreed to pass on the message.

※

Some hours later, after Anna had finished breakfast, fed Sylvia, played with the cat (who had discovered the fascination of a piece of string), and spent some time in her bedroom with a certain item over which she dreamed and mused and tried to make decisions, it occurred to her that the morning was gone and the afternoon had advanced with no sound of Ashley stirring.

Conscious of the daily deadline, she began to wonder if

she had made a mistake in denying the book editor's request. She had two choices. One was to wake Ashley out of some much-needed sleep.

The other was to do as Kate asked and find the latest chapter on the laptop, relaying the first line to Kate by email so she would think it had come from the author.

Another hour passed and Anna had decided. She went to the office, opened up the laptop and found the list of documents. At first this was confusing. It appeared the laptop contained the older entries at the head of the list and newer ones of Ashley's below. She scanned down from the top and was instantly stopped by something highly personal. The title was 'Anam Charaid'. It was the inscription on the ring she wore on her left hand and the twin of the one Lawren had also worn.

It was highly unlikely this had anything to do with Ashley. She hesitated for only a moment and then clicked on the title. A short document appeared.

```
I woke early with a strange feeling. It may
have been a dream half remembered.
I came downstairs so as not to disturb you
my darling. You were sleeping so soundly.
At first I thought there was something I
needed to sketch or draw but I found myself
here in the office with Morag purring on my
knee and the laptop waiting.
So this is a message for you that relieved
my mind of some obscure worry.
What do I need to say that had to be
written now?
Just that I love you my Anna. Always have.
Always will.
That's it. That's everything.
Now I can go back to bed. I'll erase this
```

in the morning when I've said it to you in
person my darling.

Anna knew at once the message was from Lawren. It had the mark of his writing style. He rarely bothered with punctuation or long sentences. He always insisted his words and emotions were expressed in his art.

She started to look for the date when it was written, but stopped quickly. The date was irrelevant. What mattered was that the note existed at all. It was something she could read when her feelings of loss were at their deepest and from it draw comfort. She sat back in the chair amazed that she had not dissolved in tears. Not that it was lacking in poignancy. It was a personal message, private and special, like a bird feather floating down from the sky to land right at her feet.

In place of tears she had a warm glow in her heart. This was proof of how exceptional Lawren Drake truly was. Only he would think of leaving a note for some future time. She believed he had chosen not to erase it and now, at last, she had found his message.

She decided to keep this to herself. It was another sign of confidence in her decision to share her story in Ashley's book. No matter how much she permitted to be included, there would never be all of her memories and private moments. Those she would cling to forever.

She clicked back to the documents list just as a door opened behind her.

"Aunt Anna! I thought you must have gone out somewhere. I have slept far too long but I do feel better for it. Did you need the laptop for something?"

"No Ashley! But your editor, Kate, called earlier. She is anxious to get the first line of your latest chapter for some reason. I think you should do that right away, my dear."

Ashley rubbed sleep from her eyes and became focused on what she needed to do. Anna went off to make her coffee and toast. It looked as if she would spend the rest of the day glued to the computer which gave her aunt a space of time to formulate a plan. But first, she would deal with the item she had recovered from a box in the cedar closet and which now lay in a drawer in the master bedroom.

It was a cream-coloured, three-quarter length dress with long sleeves, flaring at the wrist. The neckline was a simple scoop and the only ornamentation was a border of pattern along the hemline. She unfolded it lovingly and brought the fabric to her nose, inhaling any possible scent of the only time it had ever been worn. The reason this dress had been relegated to storage for so long was to protect it from prying eyes, and also to prevent its owner from the inevitable mix of tears and joy it aroused.

For the first time, Anna felt able to extract the joy and ignore the tears her wedding dress invoked.

It was more evidence that unburdening herself of some of her private memories allowed her to cherish the rest without fear.

She passed the border of the dress through her hands and relished the intricate design. On one of their many trips into the Scottish countryside, they had stopped for tea in a roadside café and craft shop and after enjoying the meal, they had, as was usual, browsed through the crafts on offer. Lawren had found the woven strip of fabric in muted colours depicting a family of ducks sporting on a river. He immediately purchased it saying, "This is definitely meant for the future Mrs. Lawren Drake."

Anna had laughed but she did not know how seriously Lawren had meant his comment. He had contacted one of the most talented seamstresses of the A Plus Scottish Knitters team and requested a dress to be made for Anna, to his specifications. She knew nothing of this until she had agreed to the time and place of their wedding, at which point, Lawren had presented her with the completed item.

Of course, it was a perfect fit, not only in size but also as a demonstration of his desire to make the occasion one they would cherish forever.

She smoothed the fabric and refolded it in tissue paper. It would remain in the drawer where she could see it at any time she wished. No one would ever use her bedroom again while she lived, but she would add a note to the slim package so that Ashley would understand the significance of the dress. It would rest undisturbed until then.

Next on Anna's agenda was the plan she had begun to form when it became apparent that her niece's book project was going to be published very quickly. It seemed to Anna this was an occasion to be celebrated in style and she was ready to do so.

It required a number of phone calls to ascertain the willingness of several parties to fall in with her ideas. This took considerable time and effort but the unanimous reception was positive and so she continued.

Chapter Twenty-Two

"Jean! Where are you? I've just had the most remarkable phone conversation. I have to tell you about it."

Jean was sitting on her balcony overlooking English Bay, contemplating the wonderful sea view on Canada's West Coast and wondering whether the view of the sea from her daughter's home in Oban would compare.

"I'm out here, Valerie. Come and join me."

Her friend arrived somewhat red of face and with a look of surprise that caught Jean's attention.

"Goodness! I hope it wasn't bad news about the family."

"No. Quite the opposite! You remember when I told you about meeting Anna Drake and her friend Alina and her husband who live near me in London?"

"Yes, of course. You were quite impressed with both women and you said you had an instant connection with Anna at her wonderful Scottish house on one of your tours. I have often wished to see that house. Jeanette talks about Anna all the time."

"Well, Jean, I believe you are about to get your wish."

"That's not too surprising as I am on my way to Scotland very soon. What's got you so excited, Valerie Westwood?"

"The call was from Anna Drake herself. She is asking

when you are arriving and wants to know if I can travel with you and we can make a stop in London and pick up Alina and Philip on the way."

"What? Why would we go to all that trouble? It's quite enough disruption packing my belongings to leave Vancouver forever without all the stops in between."

"Just wait until I finish and then tell me if it's worthwhile! Anna Drake is planning a big surprise.

She remembered I usually spend time in England with Zoe and Wesley after Christmas each year and she wants me to come to Oban with you before I go south."

Jean interrupted. She was finding it hard to understand the necessity for this complicated plan.

"But why do we have to collect Alina and her husband?"

"Alina has poor eyesight and can't travel without help. Philip will help as much as he can but with four of us watching out for each other we should manage better on the journey and it will be an advantage for you too."

"Now, how do you figure that Val?"

"Just listen. To start with, we get a break from the long journey in London. We can stay in Anna's condo which is closer than mine. This is a fabulous opportunity to see the exclusive paintings of Lawren Drake that are rumored to decorate the walls of their condo. It's right beside Alina and Philip's.

And, Anna suggests Alina and Philip will give you space in their baggage allowance so you can take more of your personal belongings over to Scotland.

We get a nice overnight stop, meet Alina and Philip, he's Anna's half-brother by the way, and then set out fresh the next day, by limousine, to Toronto for the last leg of the flight. A car will collect us in Glasgow. What's not to like?"

Jean, whose plans had been set for the last four months, as she thought, took some time to adjust to this new, more complicated journey.

"But, my luggage was going via Air Canada all the way to Glasgow so I don't have to handle it."

"We won't change that. I'll take an extra case for you and we'll attach Alina's tags in London.

We were going to say goodbye at the Vancouver airport and travel separately, Jean dear. You, to Glasgow, and me home to London, Ontario. This way we travel together and also help Alina. Anna has invited me to come to the celebration in Oban so we'll be together much longer than we thought."

"Oh, I'm being an old stick-in-the-mud. I was quite worried about flying such a great distance on my own and I didn't want to confess it. Now it will be much easier for me. When does Anna want us to arrive?"

"That's the best part. We can leave whenever we want in the next two weeks. We will both stay with Jeanette in your new spacious bedroom, and the other couple will stay with Anna. I just have to coordinate our flights with Philip. Doesn't it sound like a good idea?"

"I guess so. None of us is getting any younger. There's something to be said for safety in numbers at our age!"

"Michelle, it's Anna. How is Simon?"

"Oh you know your brother, Anna. He's like a bear with a sore head, complaining about every little thing and anxious to get fully active again."

"Sorry to hear that, Michelle. I know what a monster he can be when he's confined to the house. Is his hip giving him trouble still?"

"Not really. I think he just got used to complaining while he waited for the operation and now he doesn't know how to stop!"

Anna couldn't help laughing out loud at this description of her brother. It was her considered opinion no one, other than the long-suffering Michelle, could have put up with him for so long.

"Anyway, tell me how our Ashley is getting on with the book. She hasn't called in an age and I haven't wanted to interrupt her. Donna says she is working feverishly to a deadline."

"Hmm …..quite an apt choice of words, Michelle. It's Ashley I'm calling about, actually."

"Ah, she's finally tired of Scotland and anxious to get back to Prince Edward Island?"

"Not really. She's happy here for now. Did she mention her beau?"

"Now there's an old-fashioned word! Does she have a boyfriend?"

"Edmund Jansen is a doctor and not exactly in the boy category. Perhaps I shouldn't be saying anything about him at all."

"Well it could explain her long absence. What else did you want to say about Ash?"

"She has worked very hard this fall and should have her book published very soon. I want to celebrate her accomplishment and I was wondering if you and Simon would be able to come to spend New Year's over here in Scotland. It would be a bit of a party. She deserves it."

"Anna, that's a wonderful idea. We have the usual chaos over Christmas with Ken and his kids. Donna's spending the holidays with her latest 'friend.' It would really perk up Simon to have something to look forward to."

"Good! Come a day or two early. There's someone I want you to meet."

"Please include the dashing doctor as well. Donna will want to know all about her daughter's beau. It's been a long time since she had any serious romance in her life."

"I'll be sure to do that! Meantime, get your flights booked before the seats are all gone."

"Absolutely! Thanks, Anna. It will be good to see you again."

༺✿༻

"Hello, this Is Anna Drake calling. I want to invite Ross and Joyce to a New Year's party in Oban. I'll give you my contact information and ………….."

"Is that really you, Anna? I thought I recognized your voice on the answer phone message. Thank goodness I got here in time. Joyce is always saying I should let the machine take messages so we don't get interrupted all the day long, but I am so glad to hear from you."

"Ross! It's great to hear your voice again. It's been too long. You sound hale and hearty. Your retirement must be going well."

"Huh! What retirement is that? Joyce had a list of things for me to do that's miles long. I think I'm nowhere near the end of it yet. Visiting the children and the grandbairns abroad is the only break I get these days."

"I'll bet you love it all, Ross, but I have an idea for both of you to get a break over New Year's if you can come to the Oban house."

"What's the occasion, Anna? I know you've been keeping to yourself for a while now since Lawren died. Joyce and me have been giving you your privacy but that does not mean we have forgotten about you, or Simon for that matter."

"I appreciate your consideration, Ross. I am doing much better lately and I want you and Joyce to help me celebrate a new start with Simon and Michelle and our other friends, if you are free."

"Free! I would make every effort to come even if we had special plans this year. I can't wait to tell Joyce when she comes home."

"Oh, that's excellent news, Ross. I would invite you two to

stay at the McCaig Estate house like you did before, but there will be a couple there already when you arrive. My half-brother Philip and his wife Alina will be staying with me from Canada."

"Now, that's another incentive you're giving me. I feel badly that I've never met Philip in all these years. It's high time to make up for that. We are none of us getting any younger. Don't give accommodations another thought. Joyce and I will book the Highland Hotel for a few days. We'll drive up if the weather holds and we can make a holiday out of it. It's just what we need. It's going to be a grand New Year with all of us together."

"I'm so glad, Ross. You are right about time marching on. We can't afford to waste an opportunity to be together.

Have a lovely Christmas with your big family and give everyone my love.

See you soon!"

Anna sighed with relief and made a note on her writing pad where she had been keeping track of her elaborate plans for the holidays. So far, everything and everyone was falling into place. It would be a very busy couple of weeks but the house would be full of people and there would be plenty to celebrate with good friends and family.

There were still a few things to put in place for the Christmas celebration but the major decisions about who, where and how, had been checked off her list.

She thought it was fortunate that Ashley was spending so much time closeted in the office working on the book. She had no idea what was planned. Anna was quite pleased that she had accomplished it all by herself. It was high time to open up the house and open up her heart again as she had not been willing to do for so long. She had Ashley to thank for much of that willingness and soon her niece would know of her gratitude.

She looked back at the list. There was just one more thing to set in place. Call Edmund Jansen.

"Could I speak to Dr. Jansen please? It's Anna Drake calling."

"What's the medical issue, Mrs. Drake?"

"No medical issue, I'm happy to say. It's more of a personal matter."

"I see. I'll tell the doctor you called and he'll get back to you when he can."

"Thank you."

She thought this delay was inevitable so she referred to the list again and decided to make a call to the caterers to ensure everything was as she had requested. She imagined Edmund would return the call quite quickly as he had not had an opportunity to see Ashley for some time. When he saw the phone number he would think it was from Ashley.

This turned out to be the case.

"Hello. Dr. Jansen. Ashley?"

"No. This is Anna Drake."

"Is Ashley all right?"

"Oh, she's fine, Edmund. She's still very busy with her writing but I need to talk to you about a plan I have for Christmas Day. It involves Ashley."

"Mrs. Drake, I'm afraid I will be going home to spend the day with my mother. It's all arranged and I don't want to disappoint her."

"I understand." She revised speedily and found another option.

"Would it be possible for you to return to Oban in the evening for a very special occasion?"

There was a silence during which Anna's heart speeded up. Edmund must be there for Ashley.

"I suppose I could leave here on Christmas Eve and return later on Christmas Day, if you feel it's important enough for me to drive across country?"

"Yes, I do! I am sure Ashley would want you to be there

for this, but for now it's a big surprise so don't say anything about it to her."

"Not much chance of that, Mrs. Drake. I haven't seen Ashley for weeks. I don't even know what the book is about. It's certainly taking all of her time these days."

"Ah, I don't think she would mind me telling you about the book. You see it's a biography, or memoir, of my life with Lawren Drake and the book is to be released for sale by Christmas, so Ashley has a responsibility to her publisher in Canada. It's a big opportunity for a journalist, Edmund, as I think you would agree."

"Absolutely! But she should have told me."

He sounded both aggrieved and disappointed. Anna jumped in to try to calm the waters.

"Edmund, it's mostly my fault. At the start of the writing project, we did not tell anyone in case it didn't work out. I think the secrecy became a habit. You deserve to know what is happening on the evening of Christmas Day. I have arranged a Christmas feast at Glenmorie Castle for close friends and family to celebrate Ashley's achievement."

"My goodness! And you really want to include me?"

"Of course! Ashley is very fond of you, Edmund."

It's been hard for me to tell that lately. I thought she had gone off me, big time. I gave up on the idea of taking her home to meet my mother. I guess we might do it for New Year's instead, if the celebration goes as well as Anna expects.

"In that case, count me in!"

"Great! I'll be in touch with the final arrangements. Please apologize to your mother for me, Edmund."

"Somehow, I feel she won't mind too much. Thank you for including me and thank you for suggesting Fiona Campbell's cottage. Living there has made a huge difference."

"You are most welcome."

Chapter Twenty-Three

Occasionally she looked up and saw wind or rain or even snow blowing by the office window, but she was not really conscious of the amount of time that had passed since she began this regimen of work, eat, work, sleep and repeat.

By now she was inured to it and could keep going for longer writing sessions. Kate had not been too demanding about corrections or changes and yet, inevitably, several minor items escaped the author's attention, mainly because of the speed at which she was working. Those aside, Kate had agreed to leave the main thrust of the book as Ashley had wanted. If it had been necessary to revamp the entire document, Ashley felt she would have given up. Perhaps Kate sensed that too.

Warren Brady had been on the phone once to assure her she need not be concerned about the art book. Its release had been scheduled for spring in the new year. The originals had arrived safely in Halifax and been couriered immediately to Ottawa where the reaction of the arts community gave Warren every indication of an immense publication coup. Orders had already begun to flood in.

Ashley was pleased about this for her aunt's sake, but she

still worried that the arty coffee table book might overshadow her more personal work. Warren reiterated his commitment to ***A Private Couple Revealed: Anna and Lawren Drake*** and promised the publicity wheels were already turning with Indigo/Chapters planning a massive release and a newspaper campaign.

"After all, Ashley Stanton, this is a big deal in Canada. How often does one of our own reach these heights with *two*, new, important publications coming forth within months of each other?"

Ashley frequently repeated these words to herself when she couldn't sleep because her brain was humming with activity. It worked most nights but she knew she was approaching the limit of her endurance. She ran off a copy of the December calendar and taped it to the bottom of the window, taking great pleasure in crossing off a day each evening when she turned out the desk lamp.

Anna hovered nearby with coffee and sweet snacks and made sure the lounge fire was fed regularly, taking over the cleaning out of the ashes each morning. She also found a pair of suede boots with sheepskin linings for Ashley's feet. These had the effect of speeding up her output. Who knew warm feet increased blood supply to the brain?

Anna was still fielding phone calls and keeping Sylvia at bay. During the pre-Christmas season everyone was involved with shopping and family events. Jeanette was making sure everything was prepared for her mother's comfort and she was delighted Valerie would be her guest until Christmas Day was over after which she had a date in London at Dunstan's Close.

Fiona was occupied with choosing appropriate gifts for three children and Gordon, as well as being an important co-conspirator in Anna's plans.

No one arrived at the estate house for weeks except a

grocery delivery van from Tesco. Ashley heard Bev's voice in the distance once or twice but no one poked a head in to say hello, and she was grateful.

One cold day, she was typing the heading on a finished chapter when she realized she had reached chapter twenty-five. This was something of a surprise. An initial outline had proposed twenty chapters as a number to be aimed for, and now she had surpassed that without really noticing. In the way of such projects, it grew substantially as different approaches presented themselves and more involved descriptions were required. She could see the conclusion of the book in her mind. The end was nigh, for sure.

There was, however, one mighty barrier still waiting to be overcome.

Aunt Anna had not yet given final approval of the text of her story. Yes, she had read the beginning chapters before they were sent to Canada, but it had been a long time since Ashley had made the remainder available to her. In the main body of the work were the majority of the most sensitive topics which her aunt had initially approved, but which might be too revealing when seen in print with the knowledge that friends, family and complete strangers would be privy to Anna's own secrets.

It was time to correct that omission. She filled the printer with paper and ran off chapters five through twenty-four. It made a rather large stack. Ashley would continue with the final chapter while her aunt approved the main section.

It was a nervous moment when she gave the stack of pages over to Anna. There was a fierce wind blowing outside, shaking the windows occasionally. They were cozy inside the kitchen with supper dishes done and Sylvia curled up asleep in her usual position. Ashley withdrew to work for another hour or two before bed, but first she apologized to her aunt.

"I know I have left you with most of the housework around here for a long time now, Aunt Anna.

I hope that will not affect your feelings about the book. I

admit to being selfish and single-minded and I have left your final approval for far too long. It is not fair to ask you to rush through this much reading all at once, but it's too late now for me to amend my poor planning. I can only hope you are not disappointed in the results.

I will be in the office. Please come and stop me if you have any concerns."

Ashley closed the kitchen door behind her before her aunt could respond. If she had any hope of finishing the book, she would have to put out of her mind the intimidating picture of Anna Mason Drake at the kitchen table with that pile of pages in front of her. She crossed her fingers without realizing it and kept them that way until she opened up the laptop.

Ashley knew to stop writing when spelling mistakes began to appear on the page. It was a sure sign her brain was getting tired. She looked at the clock on the lower right side of the laptop screen and was astonished to discover it was almost midnight. She yawned mightily and then began to wonder if her aunt had gone off to bed. It was way past her usual bedtime.

She stood up unsteadily as blood raced down to her toes again. The room was decidedly cold. The peat fire was barely smoldering. The house was completely silent. Even the wind had ceased howling.

Panic rushed through her. Once more she had become immersed in the writing and put everything else out of her mind. What if something dreadful had happened to Anna? She remembered the time she had found Anna slumped on the chair upstairs with a high fever and the beginnings of chicken pox. That awful sinking feeling was clenching her stomach again, but this time it was related to the book pages she had given her aunt to read hours before. What if she had hated every sentence, burned the offending pages in the Aga, and stormed off to bed without saying a word? What if she could not face her niece because she was so upset and didn't want to admit it?

With so many alarming images in her mind, she could not wait a second longer to learn her fate. Throwing open the kitchen door, she stumbled inside and found Anna Drake alive, with the stack of pages in front of her on the table. Her aunt was gazing out of the bay window at the dark sky with such a look on her face that Ashley hesitated to disturb her. She was totally unable to interpret that look. Partly because her anxiety was running rampant, and partly because she had never seen such an expression before in her life.

"Aunt Anna! Are you all right?" She whispered the question, afraid of breaking the silence that surrounded her aunt like a protective bubble.

It was as if consciousness came back into her aunt's body from a place far away. Her head turned and her eyes, which had darkened to the darkest blue, cleared up and she shook her silver hair into place as she gazed at her niece.

"Don't say another word, Ashley Stanton. Sit down here by me. I have to tell you how proud you have made me by telling my story so accurately and with such compassion. If Lawren were here now, he would say the same. I read every word and I am so impressed, my dear girl."

She reached for the younger woman and there were tears in both sets of eyes; Anna's from emotion and gratitude, Ashley's from sheer relief that the final test was over."

"Are you sure? I've just finished the last chapter and I can get it for you."

"No. I never doubted you Ashley and I don't need to see another word. You have proved your integrity and discretion in so many ways. I can't thank you enough." She paused for a second.

"But there is one thing you can do for me."

"What? Anything at all! Just ask."

"I am dying for a cup of tea! All that emotion has quite worn me out."

Chapter Twenty-Four

❦

It was a Christmas feast none of the participants would ever forget.

The tall, silver candelabra marched down the centre of the Glenmorie dining table bearing aloft their white tapers. The candlelight cast a soft glow over the women's bright faces and the men's smooth cheeks.

Gordon, in full Campbell evening attire sat, resplendent, at the head of the table with Fiona facing him along its length. She wore her deep red, silk gown with the flowing skirt and looked every inch a Laird's Lady. Anna was at her right hand, with Alan and Bev Matthews on her left. Philip and Alina sat beside Anna with Edmund and Ashley opposite. At Gordon's left were the McLennans with mother-in-law Jean seated between George and Jeanette. Valerie Westwood was on the Laird's right and Callum Moir sat between Val and Ashley. The vet was a last-minute addition because Fiona insisted they could not sit thirteen people at the table without incurring bad luck. Anna and Ashley might have preferred Gregor Mackintosh but did not feel their acquaintance with him was of a sufficient length to justify inclusion.

A bright fire was burning in the grate, holly and ivy from the estate were liberally festooned on the Campbell family portraits on the wall, and the conversation flowed as freely as the rich red and white wines accompanying the five courses.

Valerie had been entertained at the Glenmorie dining table on her previous visits with select touring groups but never had she seen such splendour in her companions. Callum Moir was in his kilt and he took pains to keep his neighbour entranced with tales of his animal adventures on land and sea.

Philip and Alina were suitably impressed with the setting. The soft light was easier on Alina's eyes and her husband bent to describe in detail the relationship and dress of their dinner companions.

Ashley was entranced with everything from the wine and food, prepared and served by a trio of young people from a catering company, to the appearance of Edmund, who must have been alerted by Anna as to suitable attire for such an occasion. He wore a rented evening suit with satin lapels over a dazzling white shirt and bow tie. Ashley had never seen him in this kind of attire, or this type of company. She was both surprised and delighted with his ability to converse comfortably with everyone, including Alan and Bev. Ashley did hear him request there should be no stories about their adventure on the sheep meadow and it seemed the Matthews had agreed to respect his wishes. Edmund and Philip made a connection across the table when something was said about one of Philip's building projects in Egypt and Edmund confessed to being a follower of his work in Britain and abroad, for many years.

Jean cast happy glances over at Valerie. They had arrived in Oban several days before Christmas with time to settle into the new house. Valerie had met the McLennan children once, briefly, in the Lake District in England and she was happy to see them interacting with their grandmother who was now to be a daily part of their lives. Valerie would travel by plane to London on Boxing Day so she was careful about how much she ate and drank and made up for it with sparkling anecdotes about her travel guide adventures.

Anna squeezed Fiona's hand on top of the table from time to time. Although Anna had been the instigator of this event it was Fiona who had added the finishing details.

Donald had been given charge of Liam, Annette, Fergus and Shona and the children had a sleepover planned in the eco house after spending time earlier, trekking through the forest to see the otter family fishing in the river and having a porch cookout with burgers, fish and turkey as choices. Cameron, who was the designated driver for the evening, had been persuaded to perform his star turn of acting all the main parts in an abbreviated, Scottish version of *A Christmas Carol*, on condition the four children went speedily to sleep thereafter. Fergus and Liam competed to be Tiny Tim, while Annette and Shona claimed the parts of all three ghosts, conspiring together to get the voices right. Cameron made a video of the children's performances which was later to be a starring item in all future family gatherings.

Neil was sleeping in the old master bedroom upstairs with a heater going and a baby monitor by his side which allowed Fiona to hear every sound he made.

All the traditional Christmas meal specials were served but after the cloutie dumpling adorned with flaming brandy appeared, the three servers entered to recorded pipe music bearing a silver platter on which lay a splendid cake inscribed with *Congratulations Ashley on Your First Published Book*.

Everyone clapped and cheered, then toasted the author with champagne.

Ashley was astonished. Her head was in a spin while the congratulations washed over her from all parts of the table. She looked across at her Great-Aunt Anna who had orchestrated most of this amazing evening and her heart was full. Her head, however, was conscious of the debt she owed and she stood to thank the assembled friends and family.

"Your good wishes mean so very much to me. I am overwhelmed. It would have been enough to be included in this beautiful Christmas feast in this superb castle after all the hours I have been excluded from outside events and people. But to be praised like this is more than I ever expected.

Of course, I must thank our gracious hosts tonight." Spontaneous applause greeted this sentence. Ashley let it die down while she summoned her strength.

"Most of all, tonight I must acknowledge my debt to the lovely lady who has opened her home and her heart to me for these last months. She has been the most generous and loving of supportive companions and co-authors, while I have mined her very soul for personal, precious moments.

Without Anna Mason Drake there would be no book to celebrate. She is the true Scottish Brave Heart to me, and I owe her everything."

She only just managed to get the last sentence out without breaking down. She pushed back her chair with Edmund's help and walked over to Anna amid another round of applause and hugged her close, whispering her thanks over and over in her ear.

Ashley's speech brought a close to the evening. There were more promises of contacts and many compliments for Fiona and Gordon, especially when Neil came down in his father's arms to join the party.

George went off to check up on his brood, who he found in the eco house safely fast asleep with Donald keeping watch. Then he drove Jeanette, Jean and Valerie, home to Oban. He had indulged in only one glass of wine and stayed long enough to share the coffee that was presented for those who wished it.

Anna relaxed in the front seat of Hamish's large car with Alina by her side, while Alan, Bev, and Philip piled into the back. She had not been surprised when Ashley whispered she was going home to the cottage with Edmund.

All the way home to the McCaig house, Cameron regaled them with the antics of the four youngsters, and the car rocked with laughter. "It wouldna surprise me one little bit if that minx Annette doesn't turn out to be a grand wee actress one day. You mark my words!"

It had been a wonderful evening, worth all the careful planning, and Anna was content.

There was still New Year's Eve to look forward to but for tonight she was basking in the glow of a job well done. Her last thought, as she turned out the bedside lamp, was that Lawren would have approved.

***

The cold winter air did much to bring Ashley back down to earth. She was keenly aware of making a move to a different level in her relationship with Edmund Jansen by accepting his offer of spending the night at the cottage. The amazing evening they had shared had likely made the decision easier. She was on an incredible high for sure. Sleeping with him was not going to make up for the weeks of her neglect, but it was a fast-track to finding out if he was a one-night stand or something more meaningful.

That thought did not make it any easier to walk in the door and bounce up the stairs to his bed.

Edmund obviously felt the same way and suggested a cup of tea would be warming and provide a moment's pause for thought.

She inspected the house while the kettle boiled and was pleased to see a few personal touches added since she had last been there. Overall, the tiny place was the epitome of cozy. The contrast to the high ceilings and vast dining hall of Glenmorie Castle could not be more marked, but it suited Edmund perfectly. He did not have the time for much in the way of housekeeping chores.

They sat on the couch with their tea cups and Ashley asked a question that had been bothering her.

"Your name is not exactly Scottish. How did it come about?"

"If you agree to visit my home town, on your next Scottish trip, you can hear the whole story from my mother, but in a nutshell, it's because my father's people came to Scotland for the herring fishing, long ago. They hailed from Sweden and settled near Aberdeen to join the fishing fleets.

As to my first name…...my mother is to blame for that. She fell in love with a film star long ago. He had a glorious singing voice and she named me after him. Edmund Purdom, I believe it was. Unfortunately, I did not acquire the ability to sing, along with the name. I croak like a frog. She may never forgive me!"

The vision of Edmund trying to sing to please his mother brought Ashley to an outburst of laughter. Edmund joined in and the episode ended in a kiss.

Tea cups forgotten, they climbed the stairs together. Ashley's next question about whether he might ever consider practicing medicine in Canada, remained unasked.

Chapter Twenty-Five

All was quiet and calm in the days following Christmas, in the McCaig Estate Farmhouse.

Ashley came and went without comment, although Anna noted a gleam in her eye that had not been there previously. She was due to fly to Halifax to meet with Warren Brady before New Year's Eve and she quickly packed a case from her bedroom which had been given over to the visitors.

A package had arrived for her from her publisher and Anna placed it on the office desk for Ashley to open when she next appeared. It proved to be the first copies of *A Private Couple Revealed: Anna and Lawren Drake*. Ashley presented a copy to Anna as soon as she had autographed it and written a personal note, but Anna said she would not read it for some time yet. She needed to let the incidents settle before she delved into them again.

A copy was presented to Alina and Philip Purdy and received by them with delight. They chose also to wait, not wishing to spend one moment away from Anna in these precious few days together.

The three close friends walked when the weather was milder, talked endlessly about their lives and life decisions and ate sparingly to allow the indulgencies of the Christmas Feast to settle down.

Bev and Alan joined them for a simple meal one evening and the whole story of Sylvia and Sylvester was recounted. The female cat was now a member of the family and had been given free rein of the household. Philip did find it disconcerting to emerge from the main bathroom upstairs to find a very large cat staring at him with curiosity, but no attacks on his feet, or other parts of his person, occurred, to his great relief. Sylvia was more used to females in general although she tolerated the odd male personage who had been accepted by her owner.

Two days before New Year's Eve, a knock on the door announced the arrival of Ross and Joyce McLeod from Glasgow. A party atmosphere developed at once. The McLeods were true Glaswegians with endless entertaining tales of their large family. The constant banter between the couple revealed their affection and understanding of each other's foibles. It was a delight to listen to them.

Ross insisted on hosting the group for dinner at their hotel and drove them there while commenting on everything they passed with typical humour.

Whisky flowed freely during the fine meal and it loosened the tongues of the three siblings enough to allow them to tackle more serious topics. Alina and Joyce happily retired to a quiet corner of the residents' lounge and discussed clothes, houses, business and travel.

"Well, here we all are at last," Anna began. "Simon and Michelle will arrive tomorrow from Canada and the quartet of McLeods will be complete. Three men and one woman who have such varied histories and complicated lives. Philip was separated from his true father. Ross never knew he had another brother. Simon and I were living our lives in Canada without any knowledge of the secrets our parents' carried for so long. I don't know how the rest of you feel, but I hope you will make sure this kind of lunacy does not happen again. I think of Helen Dunlop's wasted and lonely years and I could weep. Whatever it costs in time or money, our families need to stay in touch from generation to generation. We all should tell our stories, both good and bad, and be proud of surviving to tell the tale."

She looked at the two men beside her and saw her own silvered hair on their heads. None of them knew how long they had left to live and to tell their stories.

Part of her own story was now committed to paper to be shared, and she was glad of it. Ashley had left for Glasgow airport that morning with fervent promises to return to Oban when Anna was next there.

Each McLeod held part of the story and she knew Simon, as well as their childhood friend Alina, could add more to the store of family knowledge. It was to be a grand reunion, even if delayed for too long. Anna fully intended to extract promises from these two men to meet together with Simon, in Canada, or here in Scotland, or England, or wherever it could be arranged. She would encourage Simon and Ross to bring along their children and grandchildren to keep the links strong for long after all four of the originals were gone.

In the spirit of new beginnings that Hogmanay engenders, a house full of McLeods brought in the New Year at Anna's Estate Farmhouse with traditional songs and foods. Edmund appeared shortly after the bells had rung in the new year, as 'first foot'. He carried a lump of coal as a symbol of future warmth and a 'black bun' to signify food should be ever available. Anna welcomed him in to join the party and Alan clapped him heartily on the back and approved the choice.

"There's naebody here with the required dark locks and eyes, laddie. Come awa' in and gie us your crack!"

Anna noticed whisky had caused Alan's Scottish accent to become more prominent but she enjoyed hearing all the variations on the accent that were present in her house for this night. The place rocked with noise and laughter and she recalled how Scots really know how to 'party hearty'. It was such a contrast to the months of peaceful life she and Ashley had known. She loved it for what it was, knowing the house would soon be emptied of all her guests and quiet again. Sylvia had been removed for the evening, in her cage, to Bev and Alan's farmhouse which would become her regular home until Anna returned to Oban again.

She intended to fly home to London with Alina and Philip. They would help her close up the house for the winter. Then they would take the journey in stages, staying overnight at Glasgow airport and again in Toronto since the typical Canadian January weather might cause them tiring delays. It was better to take the journey slowly and arrive in London rested.

All that remained was to say goodbye to her Oban friends, their children, and the town itself that was, in its way, also like a friend.

The next time she saw baby Neil, he would be changed entirely, but she could picture him with his brother and sister in the fine eco home his parents had built. Anna took great pride in the successful lives Fiona and Gordon had created for their family.

Jeanette, George and Jean brought their two to say farewell to 'Aunt' Anna. It was another difficult parting, especially when Jeanette saw the tears.

"Don't you worry, Anna! We'll all take care of each other for you. Remember to Skype and it won't be long until we meet again. When my two are a bit older they will be introduced to Canada with a stop in London to see you, for certain. I've instructed George to start a travel fund, now that we have a bigger house."

The plane lifted off through the cloud bank and over the islands on its westward flight.

Anna was emotionally exhausted. She always keenly felt the parting, whenever she left Scotland behind her. She did not feel like talking and she soon fell asleep with a pillow under her head.

On the adjoining seats, Philip and Alina whispered quietly for a while, then Alina reached down to her feet and removed a book from her purse.

"Well, my dear Philip, if you can do this for me, I would love to hear Anna and Lawren's story."

Her husband nodded. He knew she loved to be read to. It rested her eyes and allowed her to visualize a book's contents in a way her remaining eyesight had made impossible. In an overnight flight, he should be able to complete a good portion of the book, at least until his wife fell asleep, or he did.

He bent his head closer to Alina's ears and settled a pillow at his back.

"Ready?"

"Oh, yes!"

He began to read.

"Chapter One.

It was never to be a conventional relationship. He was a young artist with his best work ahead of him, and Anna was a partner in a thriving, online business who owned property in two countries.

That they met at all was something of a miracle.

And yet, it was to be an unforgettable and unusual love story that spanned an ocean."

THE END

The Prime Time Series concludes in *Fiona of Glenmorie*, book 8.

Afterword

Prime Time was my first series. I was hoping to find readers in the *prime* of their lives with *time* to read captivating stories, set in real-life locations and featuring women you would like to get to know.

Anna Mason is that woman. She is at a crossroads in her life when she gets a chance to take a new direction and travel to Scotland with the encouragement of her group of faithful friends.

This series is now eight full books and Anna is still going strong with adventures that will transport you to places you might never expect. You will fall in love with Anna, as I have.

Read Ruth's other series, Seafarers, Seven Days, Home Sweet Home, Journey of a Lifetime and Starscopes at retailers everywhere. Also read Borderlines a stand-alone thriller.

www.ruthhay.com

Also by Ruth Hay

Prime Time Series

Auld Acquaintance

Time Out of Mind

Now or Never

Sand in the Wind

With This Ring

The Seas Between Us

Return to Oban: Anna's Next Chapter

Fiona of Glenmorie

Seafarers Series

Sea Changes

Sea Tides

Gwen's Gentleman

Gwen's Choice

Seven Days Series

Seven Days There

Seven Days Back

Seven Days Beyond

Seven Days Away

Seven Days Horizons

Seven Days Destinations

Borderlines (Standalone)

Borderlines

Home Sweet Home Series

Harmony House

Fantasy House

Remedy House

Affinity House

Memory House

Journey of a Lifetime Series

Auralie

Nadine

Mariette

Rosalind

Starscopes Series

Starscopes: Winter

Starscopes: Spring

Starscopes: Summer

Starscopes: Fall

Made in the USA
Columbia, SC
19 October 2020